Protecting Miss Darcy

Protecting Miss Darcy

A Pride and Prejudice Variation

LEENIE BROWN

LEENIE B BOOKS
HALIFAX

Cover design by Leenie B Books. Images sourced from Deposit Photos and Period Images.

ISBN (print) 978-1-989410-64-6; (ebooks) 978-1-989410-63-9(mobi), 978-1-989410-62-2(epub)

Contents

Dear Reader,

Once upon a time...well, actually, a few years ago, I began a weekly writing exercise on my blog (lee-niebrown.com) and called it Thursday's Three Hundred. What was supposed to be just a few minutes of practice – just three hundred words a week – quickly took on a life of its own and became something much grander.

Those writing exercises have now produced several published works, including the one you hold in your hands.

While some things about how I create these stories have evolved since that first writing exercise, the tradition of posting a portion of a story continues each Thursday. In fact, there is probably a story posting there now.

Prologue

[June at Brookefield, Lord Matlock's estate]

"I am flattered that you would ask for my assistance, but..." Alfred Langley held out a well-worn piece of folded paper in Georgiana Darcy's direction.

He was going to refuse her. She could see it in his eyes and hear it in his voice. Panic filled Georgiana's breast. She needed him to accept her offer. Her friend's happiness depended upon it nearly as much as her own peace of mind did.

"Do you not wish to see your cousin happy?" she asked before he could voice his refusal.

He smiled, and Georgiana took a moment to admire his lovely blue eyes, as well as the dimple on his right cheek. It would truly not be hard to pretend to be enamoured with such a handsome gentleman. Indeed, she would likely not need to pretend – at least, not for very long. Mr. Alfred Langley was as handsome as he was kind.

"My cousin is happy. Excessively so." He waggled the paper he held. "I cannot be part of the scheme you propose, but I can assure you that I will not mention it to anyone." Again, the missive he held flapped in front of her.

"You must. Please. I promise it will only be for a short time, and then I will decide we do not suit, and you can be on your way." She drew deliberate breaths as she attempted to quiet her racing heart. How was she to face a ballroom full of gentlemen who knew who she was and what fortune she held without someone to stand between her and them?

"But I would have to lie –"

"You would be playing a part. It is only an illusion – a bit of theatre – nothing more." She struggled to keep the desperation she felt out of her voice.

"It would have to lie to everyone I love, as well as to everyone you love." He shook his head. "It is more than a play. When I attend a play, I know that what I am watching is not real. This," he waved the paper he held once again, "is a lie. No one but you and I would know that it was not real."

"Then do not pretend." She swallowed, and her cheeks grew warm. "Court me."

His head tipped as he studied her in silence. She held her breath while she waited for his reply.

"I cannot," he replied softly. "I do not intend to marry for some time. I do not even have a living. What man offers for a lady when he does not have the means to provide for her? I am certain your brother would not approve of such a match either." He paused. "Added to those rather obvious points, there is the fact that I will need a wife who is equal to my profession."

"I could be a parson's wife." She was not entirely certain she really could be, but how hard could it be to oversee a parsonage? She had been trained to run an estate the size of Pemberley.

"A parson's wife does not propose a deception."

She snatched the paper from his hands, anger at his finding her wanting rose within her. "What I proposed was a means of helping my friend and your cousin find happiness. I am certain a parson's wife cares for the happiness of her husband's parishioners to the point of putting herself out."

"Honestly," he retorted.

"I have been honest with you." Mostly.

His beautiful eyes and lovely dimple taunted her. "With me, yes. But with everyone else? No, you have not been."

She turned away from him. "Very well, then I shall have to find someone else who is more willing to help me." Where she would find another gentleman who seemed so safe as Mr. Alfred Langley, she was not certain. However, she could not let him think that he was the only gentleman to whom she could turn for help – even if he was.

"Miss Darcy, please, try to understand. I cannot place myself in the middle of a deceptive scheme. I am to be a parson. I am to be the person others look to for guidance." She heard him exhale heavily. "Imagine the difficult position I would be in if I am fortunate enough to gain the living your uncle holds, and then, he discovers I have not been honest with him."

That made sense. Her shoulders sagged. "You are right. I should not have asked this of you, but you seemed so... safe." She heard two footsteps and knew that he stood just behind her.

"How am I safe?"

She turned toward him but did not lift her gaze

from the ground to meet his eyes. "You are not a fortune hunter who would use me ill."

"Ah. The reason for the promise Miss Bennet made to you – am I right? Someone used you ill and now you are uncertain of whom to trust so you have enlisted your friend's help."

She glanced at him and smiled. "You possess a quick intellect."

"Too quick, if you ask my mother," he said lightly, causing her to chuckle. "Walk with me." He extended an arm to her. "It will make our discussion appear more natural if you do." He tilted his head toward where her brother and his wife had just entered the path he and Georgiana were on in Brookefield's gardens.

Georgiana tucked the missive she held into her pocket and took his arm.

"Now, tell me how – other than by courting you – I might be of assistance."

"You cannot be." She sighed. "Kitty will not see her promise to me as complete until I am courting or married to someone of good character. Therefore, her happiness and that of your cousin will not be so great as it could be until then – or the end of the season, whichever should happen first."

"If you are so fearful of the season, why have one?"

"It is expected."

"But surely your brother would understand if you wished to postpone your come out or preferred not to take your season in town."

"You cannot tell him." She glanced over her shoulder towards her brother. "He suffered for so long over me. I cannot be the cause of worry for him again."

"Forgive me, but I do not fully understand what you are saying." They had come to a crossroads in the path and had paused before making a choice about which way to go.

Georgiana looked first to her right and then to her left. They could take one of the diverging paths, continue on as they had been, or return to the house. She dropped Mr. Langley's arm and turned to look behind her. Retreating would be the most comfortable course for she was familiar with it. It did not hold any uncertainty, but it was surrounded by the ghosts of the past. Those secrets begged her to return to their embrace.

"I can trust you, can I not?" she asked after

stooping to pick a flower and turning back toward him.

"Completely."

"You would not lie about that would you?"

He shook his head.

"Then, we should take the path to the right as it is the longest, and my tale about my visit to Ramsgate two years ago could take some time."

Chapter 1

[August at Ravincot Hall, Lorcan Langley's home]

"We could have waited inside." Alfred Langley smoothed a hand down each sleeve and then gave a tug on the front of his waistcoat to remove any bunches and gathers which might be there.

"*You* could have waited inside, but I could not," his cousin, Lorcan Langley replied. "In fact, you could have stayed at your own home. There is really no need for you to be here."

Alfred ignored the smirk his cousin sent his direction. "I did not wish for Miss Darcy to be lonely. I know that as soon as you and Miss Bennet are reunited, you will think of little else besides each other."

"I am not so heedless as that," Lorcan protested.

Alfred laughed.

"Besides, my mother is available to entertain Miss Darcy when I am not," Lorcan continued

This time as he laughed, Alfred shook his head. "Your mother is nearly a stranger to Miss Darcy. It is much better if she has a friend to help ease the acquaintance along." He knew how Georgiana felt about meeting new people. It was just one of the many things which he and she had discussed during their fortnight together at Brookefield before she had departed for Pemberley and he had returned home.

"She will also have her brother and his wife in addition to my mother. Are you certain that helping Miss Darcy feel at ease is the only reason you are here?"

"Yes." A bit of heat touched his ears. Alfred would not deny to himself that he found Miss Darcy attractive, but he would to anyone else who asked him. He would also not deny to himself that he was looking forward to spending time with her because he found her charming, but again, he would not share that bit of information with anyone else either. He was not in the market for a wife. Therefore, Miss Darcy was nothing more to him than a charming and beautiful friend. *Charm-*

ing and beautiful friend, he repeated to himself. *Nothing more*.

His cousin stepped forward as Mr. Darcy's carriage drew to a stop in front of Ravincot Hall. A footman put the steps in place and opened the door. Mr. Darcy alighted and helped his wife from the vehicle. Then, Lorcan assisted his betrothed, Kitty Bennet, before Alfred stepped forward and offered his hand to his charming and beautiful friend.

"Mr. Langley!" Georgiana cried. "This is a delightful surprise. I had not thought to see you for at least another week."

"I thought you might welcome an extra friend, especially for those times when your travelling companions might forget you are with them."

Georgiana giggled. "Such as now?"

Lorcan and Kitty stood to the side, whispering together and looking blissfully unaware that anyone else might be around them. Alfred did not mind seeing his cousin so smitten with his lady, truly he did not, but that did not mean he would not take the opportunity to tease him about it, even if Lorcan was unaware that he was being teased.

"I have not forgotten you are here, Georgiana," Mr. Darcy said. "Nor shall I, Mr. Langley," he added with a hint of a warning in his tone.

Alfred chuckled. "I should hope not. However, I dare say Miss Bennet might." He smiled at Mr. Darcy. "And that is a good thing, is it not?"

He would have to find a moment to speak with Mr. Darcy later and assure the man that he and Georgiana were merely friends and naught else. Alfred needed to establish himself in his profession before he could consider looking for a wife. Therefore, there was no need to court anyone at present. Georgiana was just his charming and beautiful friend. Yes, he must remember that.

"Whether my husband thinks so or not, I must agree with you."

Alfred enjoyed the way Mrs. Darcy often offered her own opinion without waiting to see what her husband's would be, and from the look on Mr. Darcy's face, Alfred's admiration was in good company.

"Both you and my wife are correct, at least, to a point, and since Miss Bennet and Mr. Langley have not seen each other in a month, I cannot fault his inability to remember his duty." The man's lips twitched with amusement.

"Lori," Alfred called to his cousin, who was still whispering about something with Kitty.

Lorcan turned toward him. "Yes?"

Alfred said nothing, deciding instead to enjoy the amusement of waiting to see how long it would be before his love-struck cousin would remember to welcome *all* of his guests to his home. It did not take long, and Alfred had to bite back a laugh when the moment of realization struck. Lori's eyes grew wide, and a sheepish expression suffused his face.

"Kitty assures me that your trip was good and that there were no delays or mishaps," Lorcan began. "However, I am certain you are anxious to settle into your rooms and refresh from your journey." He motioned to the house and then, with Kitty on his arm, led them in.

"Are your aunt and uncle well?" Alfred asked.

He knew that the Darcys had planned to stop at Brookefield yesterday. The distance between Ravinscot and Pemberley was not so far that it could not be travelled in one day, but having such a lovely place as Brookefield at which to stop so that one could break up a journey into smaller pieces was no hardship and worth the extra day it would add.

"Yes, they are. Lady Matlock has made me promise that I will write to her as soon as I have arrived at Netherfield so that she can hear all the details of our trip."

Alfred motioned for her to enter the house ahead of him.

"And your family is also well?" Georgiana asked as she stood just inside the entrance hall, waiting for him to join her.

He handed his hat to a footman. "They are, though Ellen – she is my brother's wife if you remember –"

"I do," she assured him as she placed her hand once again on his arm.

He smiled. It still amazed him how quickly he and Georgiana had fallen into an easy friendship with each other. It was not that he ever truly struggled with forming friendships, but usually, and most especially with a lady, it took longer than the few weeks he had known Georgiana for the friendship to become so familiar.

"Ellen is finding the warmth of the summer to be trying."

"But she is well?"

He nodded. "She is just anxious to have her child born. She is hale and hearty. There is no need to fear."

"I am happy to hear it," Georgiana said with a small smile. "You said the baby is expected next month, did you not?"

"Yes, right before Michaelmas is what Ellen has been told." Which was just after he would be expected to take up the living at Brookefield.

"And your niece and nephew, are they looking forward to their new brother's or sister's arrival?"

"You cannot have a conversation with Lily without the baby's arrival being part of it, but Nathaniel seems rather unimpressed by the prospect. I think he is just concerned that he will have two little sisters." He laughed. "Nate takes his position as older brother very seriously."

"Oh, that is so sweet. In my opinion, there is nothing better than a caring older brother," Georgiana whispered as they entered the drawing room where Lorcan had begun introducing his guests to his parents.

Alfred knew it would be some time before he would once again be able to engage in conversation with Georgiana. The thought was rather disappointing, but it was how things must be.

There were the usual pleasantries of greeting and then the showing to rooms that had to be done. After that, a light meal was had on the terrace, and then, finally, the newness of the arrival of guests began to dissipate and was replaced with a more relaxed familiarity.

And then. Ah, and then, as the ladies and Lorcan toured the house with Alfred's aunt and as Alfred's uncle returned to his study to have a discussion with his steward who had just arrived, Alfred found himself alone in the billiards room with Mr. Darcy.

"I wished to speak with you," Alfred said as Darcy lined up his first shot.

Darcy glanced up at him. "About Georgiana?"

"Yes."

The sound of billiard balls knocking together punctuated the silence that followed Alfred's answer.

"She is not yet officially out," Darcy said with a pointed look.

"I know. I do not wish to speak to you about courting her."

Darcy leaned against the table with his cue resting against his chest and his arms folded around it. "You do not?"

"No, quite the opposite."

"I am not sure I understand."

Not since he had been taken to task by his father over the moving of his brother's clothing, which had led to Edgar's forced betrothal, had Alfred witnessed such an intimidating look as the furrowed brow and scowl Mr. Darcy was currently wearing. Alfred had made it a goal to not be put in such a position again if it could at all be helped, and, until this moment, he had succeeded.

"I wished to assure you that she and I are merely friends."

Darcy's eyebrows rose. "Merely friends, you say?"

"Yes, friends."

Darcy stepped away from the table and allowed Alfred to take his shot. "You seemed rather eager to see her when we arrived today, and I must admit that I was surprised to find you here."

Alfred could clearly hear the implication of the

man's words. "I came in the office of a friend to provide a service."

"Again, you will need to explain that if you wish for me to believe it."

This was not going at all how Alfred had imagined this discussion would go. He had imagined Mr. Darcy to be a more understanding sort of fellow and not so given to suspicion. But, then, Alfred did know how Georgiana had been played upon by someone her brother had trusted, so he supposed it only stood to reason that Darcy should be cautious.

"I can explain it so long as you do not let on to your sister that you know of this. I swear it is nothing indecent or improper," he hastened to add when Darcy's eyes narrowed. Yes, facing his angry father was less terrifying than he imagined Mr. Darcy could be when utterly put out. "Your sister confided in me, while she was at Brookefield, that she sometimes finds it challenging to enter a new situation without a certain amount of anxiety – more anxiety than one might expect. I understand there are reasons for such apprehension, one being her natural bent and the other being her unfortunate experience."

Darcy lowered his stick which had been poised to take a shot. "How exactly did you come to understand this?"

"Your sister explained it to me." Alfred felt as if Darcy's stare was going to burn a hole through him.

"She told you about..."

"Ramsgate," Alfred said.

Darcy expelled a great breath.

"She did not wish for you to be worried about her, but the thought of a season terrifies her."

"She told you all this?" Both of Darcy's hands rested on the edge of the table, propping him up while his gaze was directed at the surface of the table. It was almost as if the man were straining against a great physical weight.

"Yes, and that is why I am here. She does not know my aunt and uncle, and neither do you and your wife. Therefore, since I knew that Lori would be of little use in making her arrival and introduction to an unfamiliar setting easy, I came to offer my service in the matter."

Darcy's head shook, and Alfred dared to go stand next to the man.

"I mean her no harm," he said softly. "I wish only for her comfort."

"Why?" Darcy's tone was equally as soft. "Why did she tell you this and not me?"

The image of a letter asking Alfred to pretend to court Georgiana filtered through his mind. That missive was the inciting element, but it was not the reason. Therefore, he pushed that to the side and said, "She does not wish to burden you again."

"But it is my place to bear her burdens."

"I will not deny that," Alfred replied. "However, it is not yours alone to bear. She must also be allowed to seek assistance from her friends."

Darcy shook his head. "She has known you for such a short time."

"But she sees me as safe, and, in that, she is not mistaken. She and her secret will always, *always*, be safe with me."

Darcy stood and paced a circle halfway around the table before stopping and leveling a serious look at Alfred. "You would do well to marry an heiress. It is what your mother wishes."

"I am not pretending to be her friend to some-how coerce her into marrying me so that I can have her money." Alfred knew his tone was less than civil, but if there was one thing that caused him to lose his hold on his emotions, it was being accused of being duplicitous. "I loathe deception."

Darcy continued to look at him with the same intense expression. "Then, you do not find her attractive?"

A small burst of laughter escaped Alfred. "I am not blind, but as you said, she is not yet out and, as I keep repeating to those around me, I am not yet ready to contemplate marriage. Your sister will be safely married before I am even at such a point." That was a thought that was not so comforting to him as he hoped it was to her brother.

"Only friends, you say?"

"Yes. Your sister is merely my friend." His beautiful, charming friend.

"And she is safe with you?"

"I would protect her with my life if needed."

Darcy studied him for one more long, silent moment. "Very well, I shall believe you. However, I expect you to be as circumspect as can be when with her, and, should my faith in you prove to be misplaced, I will see you pay."

"And I should hope that you do." Alfred's gaze

held Darcy's without wavering until Darcy nodded.

"So long as we understand each other then."
And with that, Darcy turned his attention back to
the game they were playing.

Chapter 2

My dearest aunt,

We have arrived safely at Ravincot Hall, and it is just as lovely as you described it to be. Mrs. Langley is all that is gracious. I find it particularly wonderful how she has accepted Kitty as if she were already her daughter and has been for some time. I can see now why you thought it a good plan to write to her regarding the match and the trouble arising from Wes and Mary's wedding breakfast. I can also see how my fears about the scheme were unfounded. She is most certainly a doting mother if ever there was one – nearly more doting than you are, but not quite. I am not certain there is a mother or aunt in all this world who can love the children trusted to her care as you do.

To my delighted surprise, it was not just one Mr. Langley who greeted us upon our arrival but two! Mr. Alfred Langley has made the trip to Ravinscot from his home, *and he plans to stay a few days before returning home and preparing for our visit to his estate.*

I will admit this to you so long as you do not mention it to my brother. It was a relief to see a familiar friendly face when first stepping out of our carriage. It took little more than a smile and warm greeting to stop my heart from fluttering at the prospect of being in a place wholly unfamiliar to me. I fear the prospect of the season pressing upon my mind has given rise to nerves that are more easily aroused. I shall be glad when the day of the assembly in Hertfordshire arrives so that my excitement and trepidation can be put behind me. As you always say, it is often just the anticipation of waiting that is most unsettling.

Georgiana was not entirely certain about how true her aunt's words were, but, with each passing day, she was growing more assured of her ability to face her season with graceful composure, and therefore, she would accept her aunt's words as true for now.

Alfred – her lips curled in pleasure – she had finally come to a place where she could think of him so familiarly without blushing. Alfred had been the perfect gentleman with whom to start her study of character. If she could find a gentleman, who was as honorable and amiable as Alfred, but who was not a parson, to fall in love with her, she knew her future would be the happiest it could possibly be.

The door opened, putting an end to Georgiana's reflection. Quietly, Kitty slipped into the room she was sharing with Georgiana as Georgiana added a closing to this portion of her letter.

I shall write again when we get to Winsdale Court.

With all my love,

Your devoted niece, G

"Has Mr. Langley allowed you to leave his side so soon? The moon has barely made an appearance," she teased before blowing gently on her missive to dry the ink.

Kitty blushed. "He did not wish to, but I did not want to leave you alone."

"I would have been fine by myself. I was just beginning my letter to my aunt, and I have a book to read."

Georgiana tucked her pen, ink, and letter into her travelling desk. It was sweet of Kitty to think of her, but she did not want her friend to feel as if she was required to entertain her.

"I think Mr. Alfred Langley missed having you

to play that last hand of whist with him." Kitty looked up from her task of removing her stockings.

Georgiana knew that look. It was the one she had seen Kitty use many times when suggesting that Alfred would be a good match for Georgiana.

"He is just a friend. No matter how much you would like for us to be cousins, as well as sisters, he is just a friend."

Part of her wished she could consider Alfred as more than a friend, but the more logical portion of her brain knew that it was not possible. She was not what Alfred wished for as a wife.

"A very handsome friend," Kitty prodded.

Georgiana could not deny that. Alfred possessed just the right height and broadness, as well as the most perfect shade of dark brown hair. His eyes were expressive and often laughing; and when he smiled, the most delightful dimples would appear. A lady could not ask for a more handsome friend. "It would be dreadful if gentlemen could not have friends unless they were *not* handsome."

Kitty giggled. "That would, indeed, be horrible."

"He is only my friend," she repeated to herself and Kitty. "He is more like a brother than anything else."

Drat! She had not yet mastered the ability to say such a thing without her cheeks colouring. Of course, the disbelieving look Kitty gave her was not helping her feel at ease about such a falsehood.

However, it was pointless to think of Alfred in any other way. He was to be a parson and needed a lady who could fill the role of a parson's wife to perfection. She was not that lady. Had she not nearly fallen victim to a rogue and, in so doing, had she not schemed to keep her attachment to the man a secret to the point of nearly eloping? And then, just a little over a month ago, had she not presented another scheme based on being untruthful to Alfred?

He had been right. She had not wished to admit it at the time, for it stung to be found wanting, but that is exactly what she was – wanting. She did not have the sort of character that a parson's wife required. After all, deception was not listed among the things of which God – or parishioners – approved.

Her conscience pricked her, but the lie she had told Kitty could not be avoided. With any luck, it would soon not be a lie at all but rather the truth. Alfred would eventually become just like a brother and not cause her to think of being held in his arms whenever he did something sweet such as he had today by being at Ravincot when she arrived so that she would not be lonely. If she just repeated it to herself often enough, it would, with time, become reality. It had to.

"I will ring for our maid, and then, once we are in bed, you can tell me all about your first impressions of your new home and family."

"I am not certain it has fully set in that this will be my home in the future." Kitty sighed. "Is it not wonderful?"

Georgiana could only smile and agree. While the house and grounds of Ravincot were lovely, if you asked Georgiana, the happiness in Kitty's expression when talking about her future was the most wonderful part.

"We shall have to do our best to find you a gentleman who has an estate that is not too far from here," Kitty added just before their maid entered. "I will be very sad if you are too far from me."

"That may not be possible." Though Georgiana wished it was. She had never had a friend so dear as Kitty.

Again, Kitty sighed. "Brookefield is not so very far from here."

"I do not see how that is significant."

"Do you not?" Kitty asked with a flutter of her lashes.

Oh, Georgiana knew exactly what her friend was saying. However... "I believe we have already canvassed that topic."

"But he is handsome and of good character."

"While that is true, he is not for me." Sadly. "Maybe there will be a gentleman to my liking in Hertfordshire. That is only a day's drive from here."

"Brookefield is closer."

"Kitty!"

"Very well, I will not mention it again." Her lips tipped into an impish grin. "At least, not for the rest of today."

And to her credit, Kitty did not mention it again until they were in the garden the next day. Lorcan had been required to attend to some matter with his father, and Kitty was sitting with Georgiana in the garden while Georgiana sketched a flower. Thankfully, Lorcan had returned before Kitty could press Georgiana too far on the subject of Alfred.

When Kitty had left her, Georgiana had turned her face to the sun for a few minutes – not long enough for it to cause her to brown, but just long enough to enjoy its warmth on her cheeks and feel the delight that such brightness brought to the senses. With her face tipped up and her eyes closed, she began humming a cheery tune and continued to do so when she returned to her work.

"That is a very good likeness," Alfred said as he took the seat next to her which Kitty had vacated.

"Thank you. Flowers are my specialty." She smiled at him sheepishly. "To be honest, they are the only thing I can draw that comes close to looking as it should."

"I find that hard to believe."

"It is the truth."

"You cannot do a silhouette?"

She bumped his arm with her shoulder. "That is not the same as drawing."

"Leaves. Can you draw a leaf?"

"Yes, they are part of a flower."

He shook his head. "They are not always part of

a flower, and look here," he pointed to her page, "I believe that is grass."

"It is still just part of the garden."

"But it is not a flower. Therefore, I maintain that you are adept at drawing more than just flowers." He turned one of his brilliant smiles at her. It was the sort of smile that caused any doubts about herself to flee. Whomever she chose to marry needed to have the ability to make her feel so accepted and lighthearted with just a smile as Alfred did.

There was no other way to respond to his smile than to grin – a bit foolishly – and agree that he was right.

"You must then allow me to modify my words," she said with a light giggle, "I am only adept at drawing plants in such a fashion that they can be recognized for what they are."

"I think you could draw other things satisfactorily as well – still life items – ribbons, vases, fruit, plates, and the like."

"Are you always so stubbornly encouraging?"

Alfred laughed. "No, not always, but I have been told it is one of my best annoying qualities." He turned his whole body so that he was facing her more than he was facing the garden. "Encouragement is one of the things my mentor – Mr. Hatcher – has stressed to me as a necessary trait to cultivate."

"I cannot believe it is a trait you have only just learned, for it seems as if it comes very naturally to you."

He laughed. "I have always been the sort to look for the fun and frivolity in a situation, but I must move beyond just encouraging that which is easy. That is what I have learned – that I must temper my enthusiasm at times and consider the root of the enjoyment and the end result."

"But that is what we all must do as they grow older."

"You are not wrong. As one grows older, one learns to decipher the right from the wrong and the wise from the unwise." He tipped his head and studied her face for a moment, causing her to wish to fidget at the close scrutiny. "I will attempt to explain it without sounding too much as if I am standing behind a pulpit," he said with a smile.

"Encouraging people to do good is the easy part while encouraging them to leave sinful practices behind is more challenging. However, the most challenging, at least in my way of thinking, is encouraging faith – faith in the goodness of our God, faith that the circumstances in which an individual finds himself have a purpose, faith that the abilities and talents placed within a person were put there by their Creator – those sorts of things are sometimes beyond what I feel I can do." He shrugged. "I hope that with time and effort it will become less difficult and that I will struggle less with them myself."

"You struggle with that?" This was, perhaps, the first time Georgiana had heard a parson admit to having difficulty with faith.

He nodded. "I do." He blew out a breath and looked away for a moment. "For instance, what purpose is there in an infant losing her mother before she ever knew her? Or how can good come from a trusting young woman being duped? Sometimes the answers are not clear, and, as Mr. Hatcher would say, sometimes they are not to be found. However, Mr. Hatcher would always add that one must have faith that our God sees the reason." The smile Alfred gave her was lopsided. "I find that part to be nearly impossible to grasp because I like to know why."

"It would most certainly be nice to know why,"

she said softly. Her heart was touched that he thought of her and the things which had happened in her life when he was contemplating such weighty subjects as faith.

He took one of her hands. How did he know that such a small action would impart so much comfort?

"Perhaps, one day you will know the answers to those questions. We must believe you will."

"Or we must accept not knowing."

He sighed. "Yes. Though that is not my preference."

"Mr. Langley, Georgiana."

Alfred dropped her hand as if it had burned him. "Mr. Darcy, Mrs. Darcy," he said in greeting as he rose.

"It is a lovely day to be in the garden, is it not?" Elizabeth said.

"It is," Georgiana replied. "I was drawing." She shifted the notebook in her lap to draw her brother's attention away from Alfred.

"It is very good," her brother said with a small smile for her before turning his attention back to Alfred and scowling once again.

"I think I have had enough fresh air and sunshine," Alfred said. "Miss Darcy, thank you, for allowing me to disturb your solitude." And with a bow he was gone, leaving a very noticeable absence at Georgiana's side.

Chapter 3

What had possessed him to take her hand? Alfred rested his head on the wall against which he was leaning rather than knocking it against the plaster as he wished to do. He had never taken anyone's hand when speaking to them about a sensitive subject. Why had he done so just now with Georgiana?

Georgiana. He repeated the name and sighed. That was likely why. He thought of her in familiar – nearly familial – terms. That had to be the reason. In his mind, she was like family. A sister? He scowled. No, not a sister. One did not think about how pretty a sister was in the way he thought about how pretty Georgiana was. A cousin? His eyebrows rose as he nodded at the possibility. Perhaps a distant cousin who visited and wrote often enough that she was distant only in family connection. Yes.

Yes, that would do. She was a distant cousin, and as such, he felt at ease offering her support by holding her hand.

He grimaced. That was still a bit unacceptable, but it would have to do because his taking her hand could not be because he, unbeknownst to himself, wished for her to be more than a friend. He closed his eyes and shook his head. No, that most certainly could not be it.

He pushed off the wall next to the door to this small upstairs sitting room that was rarely used and crossed to the window to look out at the garden. The aspect was good, but on the small side, as the window was not grand. It was an appropriately sized window for the room. It just was not so large as the garden deserved. His aunt spent a great deal of time on her garden. Her gardener was one of the best in the area, and there were always small improvements, if not large ones, being done to Ravincot Hall's grounds. This smallish window did not do his aunt's work justice.

The window was large enough, however, for Alfred to see that Georgiana was still on her bench with her head lowered as she applied herself to her drawing, while, arm in arm, Mr. and Mrs. Darcy strolled the path behind her.

Again, he wished to knock his head against a wall. Not only had he held Georgiana's hand, but he had also been caught doing so by her brother. That gentleman likely believed even less now that Alfred could or would protect his sister and not toy with her heart. The idea soured Alfred's stomach.

Alfred was not opposed to an innocent flirtation with a pretty lady. There was nothing inherently wrong with the dance of admiration in which ladies and gentlemen partook as they decided whom they might pursue as a good match and companion of their future lives. However, he found the practice of some gentlemen who flirted only with the aim to seduce to be repulsive. He and Lori had argued over such things many times. Lorcan was not as likely to seduce a lady as his friend Lord Westonbury had been, but Lorcan had most certainly used his charm to steal kisses and caresses.

Thankfully, Lori was the sort of fellow who needed to feel an emotional connection to a lady to move beyond what could be stolen in a few minutes in a darkened corner. Not that Alfred would ever share that secret, which he had discovered by accident when listening to a quiet conversation between Lori and Lord Westonbury regarding a particular mistress whom his cousin had visited. There was no need to worry that his cousin would ever stray from his wife so long as he married for love.

Alfred chuckled. As if Lorcan would ever marry for any other reason! Lori was not the sort to seek to gain an advantage in wealth or position at any cost, and his parents would have been the first to attempt to prevent such a match. Alfred's aunt had been the daughter of parents who were locked in a loveless relationship. There was no way she was ever going to allow her children to be part of such a dismal life, and her husband, Lorcan's father, was far too delighted in and in love with his wife to disagree with her on such a subject.

They were blessed. Both he and Lori were blessed. Neither of them had parents who were social climbers even though Alfred's mother did often mention that he should try to find an heiress to love – she always added *to love* to her description of any lady he might decide to marry.

"The garden is best enjoyed from outside."

"I was just out there," Alfred replied. "What brings you to this room, Aunt?"

Meredith Langley crossed to stand next to her nephew. "You."

"Me?"

His aunt nodded. "We have not yet had a good discussion about my son and his future bride." Mrs. Langley sat down on the window seat so that she could also look out the window. "There is a pleasant breeze today, is there not?"

"A very pleasant one," he agreed. That was another reason he liked this room. When one left both the window and the door open, there was often a stirring breeze that would waft through this room. It was very well-situated.

"That is how I knew where to find you," she added with a little laugh. "You have always enjoyed the wind blowing gently on your face and through your hair. Nearly from the moment you were born."

Alfred had spent so much time with his cousins and aunt and uncle that Aunt Meri was nearly a second mother to him.

"Your nurse would place you on a blanket in

the garden and without fail, you would find the breeze and turn yourself towards it." She laughed. "Your mother and I thought perhaps you would be a sailor because of how you always seemed to find the wind. However, as you grew older and began walking and talking, it was as plain as plain to see that you were not meant for the navy or any other profession which would put you in the position to harm another – not even if that other person was an enemy." She drew and released a breath. "You were – and are – such a gentle spirit."

"You think so?"

She nodded. "Much as Lorcan is. You two are alike in that way. You both got into scrapes and pursued boyish pursuits with abandon." She smiled at him. "And always with a hearty laugh if you were involved." She shook her head. "I have never met a child who was so happy as you were. Lorcan was by no means a difficult child with a foul temper, but he did not smile as you did. If you could not be a gentleman farmer, your mother would say, you were meant to be a parson so you could share your light with all you served."

Alfred chuckled. "She has said that to me a time or two. I hope I do not disappoint her."

"Do you think you will?" his aunt asked in surprise.

Alfred shook his head. "Not intentionally."

"Small foibles are forgivable." Her smile turned teasing. "Just do not make any grave errors, and always keep your clothes near when swimming."

Alfred laughed at that. "I have no younger brothers. I think I shall be safe."

His aunt chuckled. "You have Lorcan and his friend Westonbury."

"Duly noted. I will not go swimming when they are present. Actually, I dare say I shall not go swimming often as it is. I think I have outgrown my years of frivolity."

She took his hand. "You are not so old as that."

"But I am a parson, and it would not do to be discovered swimming by a parishioner."

"Then save your swimming for the pond at Winsdale when you visit."

"I will."

"And take your children there to teach them. A child should know how to swim. It is the best way to keep them safe."

"I promise to teach my sons to swim."

"And your daughters," his aunt added.

"And my daughters," he said. "How many children do you think I will have?"

"A nursery full, at least. You are the sort of man who will be an excellent father." She patted the window seat next to her and he sat.

"I believe you think more highly of me than I deserve because you are my aunt."

She shrugged. "Perhaps I do, but then, again, perhaps I do not. Now, tell me, what is your opinion of my future daughter?"

"Do you truly need to know?"

She shook her head. "No, but I would like to hear you tell me I am not wrong for liking her so much as I do."

"You are not wrong. Miss Bennet is a genuinely lovely lady who loves Lorcan far more than he deserves."

"I do not think that is possible."

"Then, you understand how much he is loved by his lady."

"Ah, see. What other gentleman would say such a thing? Anyone other than you would have told me that it is entirely possible that my son is not so perfectly lovable as I like to think he is, but not you. You understand my love for my son and have used that to your advantage."

"Aunt Meri, if you do not wish for me to become arrogant, you are going to have to stop praising me at every turn."

She laughed. "You will not grow arrogant, for you do not believe half of my praise. You know yourself very well."

He wished that part of his aunt's commendations was true. He was not entirely certain he knew himself so well as he thought he did before... he turned to the window. Georgiana was once again lifting her face to the sun.

"You always did like finding the most beautiful flower in the garden," his aunt whispered.

He turned startled eyes in his aunt's direction.

"Miss Darcy. She is..." she paused and studied his face, "quite wonderful and so sweet."

"She is," he agreed. "I think I have done well to find such a *friend*."

His aunt's eyebrows rose, and she pressed her lips together as if she was attempting to contain a laugh. Maybe he should depart for home tomorrow instead of the day after. Then, maybe, it would put to rest the notions everyone had that he wished to court Georgiana.

"Miss Bennet," he said, turning the conversation back to where it belonged, "is also quite wonderful and sweet, as well as being an excessively loyal friend."

"Lorcan said something about it being Miss Bennet's not wishing to break a promise to a friend which caused the misunderstanding that sent him home in such a state as he was in."

Alfred nodded. "Miss Darcy has her come out this year, and for various reasons to which few are privy, Miss Bennet had promised to stand at her side while she made her debut. It was not a promise she was willing to break even at the cost of her own heart and desires."

"I am satisfied. My son has, indeed, chosen well, just as I thought."

"He has, and I assure you that I questioned Miss Bennet sufficiently before Lori offered for her." He turned back to the window. "Her answers were more than acceptable, but it has been the testimony of her friend which has deepened my approval from what it was at first to what it is now."

"And what is it now?" his aunt asked.

"I can think of no one I would rather claim as my cousin than Miss Bennet. Her heart is not just kind as is often said of many ladies. It is kind in the purest sense, for she does not seek to gain advantage through her kindness." He shrugged. "She is a breath of fresh air on a stale day."

His aunt cupped his cheek with her hand. "And you are the best at finding a pleasant breeze." She patted his cheek. "Are you going to remain here?" she asked as she rose.

He nodded as he turned his attention back to the garden. "I might leave tomorrow."

"Why?"

He shrugged. "I am anxious to be home." Where he could order his thoughts so that he would not feel so turned around, and where there was little chance of holding Georgiana's hand or being scowled at by her brother.

Aunt Meredith tipped her head as she looked at him with a furrowed brow. "I will be sorry to see you leave us so soon."

And he would be sorry to leave. However, it needed to be done.

"Thank you, for your reassurance that my son will be happy," his aunt said before placing a kiss on the top of his head. Then, she placed a hand on his shoulder and looked out at her garden. "Small foibles," she said, "are forgivable. Just do not make any grave errors."

He gave her a quizzical look.

"You are a smart boy. I am certain you will figure it out." Her eyes travelled back to the garden view for a moment before she moved toward the door, pausing just before she left the room to add, "And with any luck, one day, you will be just as happily matched as Lorcan."

Chapter 4

"Does it hurt much?" Kitty asked as she applied some salve to Georgiana's red nose.

"Not overly much — less than last night, and it is no more than I deserve. I know that enjoying the sun so freely as I did yesterday is not proper." She winced as she looked in the mirror. The pain of how such a red nose made her appear was greater than the stinging burn of the injury. "It looks dreadful."

Kitty said nothing, choosing instead to give Georgiana, who sat at the dressing table, a quick hug from behind.

"I will keep to the shadows today and wear my bonnet with the widest brim."

"You look lovely in any hat you wear." Kitty's head was in the wardrobe they were sharing. "You must wear this." She pulled out a blue and white striped cotton day dress. "It will pair very well with your wide-brimmed bonnet if we change a ribbon or two." Kitty fluffed the ruffles at the neckline and sleeves before checking the three rows of ruffles at the bottom of the dress. "It looks every inch the perfect dress for a picnic."

"You are very good at picking the best thing to wear," Georgiana said as she rose from where she sat. "I have always liked that dress. It will be perfect."

"Do you really think I am good at choosing what to wear?" Kitty wore a pleased smile.

"I do. Why do you ask such a thing?"

"I had not thought I was very good at fashion. However, I have learned many things from you and Lydia, so perhaps that is it."

Georgiana stopped removing her robe and stared at her friend until Kitty asked if something was amiss.

"Yes, I cannot believe you think you are unequal to the challenge of putting together a delightful ensemble. Your eye for colour and feel for fabrics is excellent."

"I am fond of colour," Kitty agreed.

"I think you just needed some direction to set

in motion the natural abilities you already possessed."

"Do you think so?"

Georgiana nodded. "A bit of confidence is all that is needed."

She paused in the straightening of her chemise. Confidence was not something easily gained, was it? She drew a breath in through her nose and exhaled slowly while putting her stays in place so that Kitty could help her tie them. A wrong choice in what one wore could be tragic to be certain, but it was not so terrible a thing as trusting the wrong gentleman was. Still, it warranted more consideration, for her trepidation about the season might not be based on a want of skill in determining character but rather a confidence in the skills she already possessed.

"What are you thinking?" Kitty asked. "Or is it your burnt nose which makes you frown? There, you are all secure."

"No, it is not my nose." Georgiana turned to render the same service in tying Kitty's stays as Kitty had just completed for her. "I was just thinking about my season."

Kitty looked over her shoulder at Georgiana. "And what about it is making you frown?"

"Do you think that my troubles stem from a willingness to believe what is not there rather than seeing what is? Or do you think my anxiety stems from a lack of faith in my abilities to determine the character of a gentleman?" She tucked the tails of Kitty's laces under the edge of the garment.

Kitty's brow furrowed. "How often have you been misled by the character of another? It was just the once with Mr. Wickham, was it not?"

Georgiana nodded.

"And what did you think of Lorcan when you first met him?"

"I liked him very much. He seemed amiable and all that was proper." She smiled. "Or, at least, so proper as a friend of my cousin can be."

Both she and Kitty laughed at that. Lord Westonbury was not known for his propriety, after all.

"I had the benefit of knowing that Mr. Langley was a good friend of Wes, and while my cousin was known to relish a good time, I also knew he did not abide fools and hateful people. Therefore, I do not know if my assessment of your Mr. Langley is a good way to judge my abilities."

Kitty stood inside her dress about to put her arm into a sleeve. "Oh, but I think it is! You made your assessment based on what you knew of Lorcan's friends and how he presented himself." She stopped and turned to face Georgiana fully, with one arm in one sleeve and one arm waiting to be placed in the other sleeve. "That is exactly what you did with Mr. Wickham as well!" She looked absolutely delighted with her declaration. "You looked to who he knew – your father and your brother – and since neither had ever spoken ill of him, why would you presume that he was anything but good? And he treated you well, did he not?"

"Yes, very, but it was an act."

"I know that," Kitty replied. "But you could not have assumed he was anything worse than what he appeared for there was no evidence of it. Even Elizabeth liked Mr. Wickham when she first met him." Kitty paused once again in getting dressed. "Although, there were some signs that he was not all that was proper. He spoke too freely on too short an acquaintance. I heard Jane say so. Still, Elizabeth chose to believe he was acceptable."

"That is because she found my brother to be disagreeable and so did Mr. Wickham." That was what Elizabeth had told Georgiana.

Kitty shrugged. "There is that, but she still was led astray, though not as innocently as you were." Her eyes grew wide. "Perhaps I should not have said it like that. It was rather critical of me to say."

"It is the truth. Elizabeth has said as much to me."

Kitty sighed in relief. "As soon as it left my lips, I knew it was not something Jane would say, and immediately thought I had spoken amiss."

"Is Jane perfect?"

"Nearly so," Kitty replied.

Georgiana laughed.

"It is true. Jane is nearly never wrong. I should very much like to be as she is."

"But you are you, and I think you are quite perfect the way you are."

Kitty smiled. "And I think the same about you."

"So then, it is my faith in myself which is lacking?"

"No," Kitty reached a hand out to fix a ruffle at Georgiana's shoulder that was standing up rather than lying down. "Your faith is not lacking but rather shaken. It needs assurance much like a lamb needs a nudge from its mother to try walking again after it falls down."

Georgiana embraced her friend. "This is why you are perfect the way you are, for you have told me exactly what I needed to hear and said it how I needed to hear it. I much prefer thinking of myself as a lamb on wobbly legs than a failure."

She could walk and stumble and walk some more. She did it as a child in leading-strings and, to this day, she rarely stumbled and fell when walking. A few leading-strings – that was what she needed. A second opinion about a person's character from her friend, her brother, Elizabeth, her cousin Richard, or... she smiled as she rang for her maid to come to fix her hair... Alfred. He seemed as wise a counselor as any of the rest of them. And she had to admit, he was the most handsome counselor she had listed. If only she was the sort of lady who would make an excellent parson's wife.

"You are frowning again," Kitty said.

"I was just thinking." She could not tell Kitty that she was pondering what qualities a parson's wife should possess.

"About what?" Kitty asked.

"It was nothing of great significance." Or, at

least, it was not at present. In fact, it was likely a poor idea. One should not attempt to be something she was not to impress a gentleman, should she?

"Are you certain?"

Georgiana nodded. It was a poor idea. She wanted a husband who loved her for who she was, and that included her shortcomings. She blew out a breath and returned Alfred to his proper place of a mere handsome friend and an excellent counselor.

"If you are truly certain..."

"I am," Georgiana said.

"Do you think the Langleys' neighbours and Lorcan's sister will like me?" Kitty asked as she took a seat so that her maid could see to her hair.

"Yes, miss. They will love you," her maid said.

"Indeed, they will," Georgiana agreed.

~*~*~

And they did. The picnic had been a success, and Kitty was currently walking along the edge of the meadow with Lorcan and his sister, Emma, while looking very much at ease.

"You look perfectly content." Alfred sat down beside Georgiana under the tree.

"I am. It was a lovely picnic."

Chairs and tables were being loaded onto a waiting cart, while blankets which were not being used, were folded and placed in a trunk that would be transported back to Ravincot in one of the Langley's carriages when they had all had their fill of wandering the meadow and reclining under trees as they conversed.

"Are you planning to sit here and read until we leave?" Alfred asked.

"That was indeed my plan unless some other activity of greater interest caught my attention."

"Would you like to walk with me?"

"I think I could be persuaded to put my book aside for such a treat."

He laughed as he rose and extended his hand to her. "I dare say you are exaggerating how much of a privilege it is to walk with me."

"Do you doubt my sincerity so much?" she teased.

"No... no..." he stammered, "that is not it at all. It is just that..." His brow furrowed as if he was not sure how to proceed.

"Can it not be a delight to walk with a friend?"

"I suppose it can be," he replied.

"Then, you must allow me to consider it a treat to walk with a friend." To her surprise, instead of causing him to smile one of his easy smiles, the comment evoked a pensive expression.

"I am going home tomorrow," he said after a few minutes of silent walking.

"Tomorrow? I thought you were staying at Ravincot for three more days."

"You seem well-settled and at ease. I do not think you require anything further."

Was that truly all he had come to do? To make certain she was settled into her surroundings and then take his leave like a parent who spends a few moments in the nursery before leaving his child with the new nursemaid.

She forced a smile to her face and attempted to insert it into her voice. "Then, this is an even greater treat since I am to be denied the pleasure for a week."

"Yes... well..." His eyes studied the ground as they walked.

"I understand your aunt has planned a few more parties to introduce Kitty to her friends."

He nodded. "So I have heard."

"And you think I will do well at each of those

without your calming presence?" Perhaps he would stay if he thought she needed him.

Again, he nodded. "You are more than adequate to the challenge."

"You are determined to go then?"

A third nod.

"Before you go, could you do one thing for me?"

"Anything."

"I heard mention that there may be an unattached gentleman or two included in these groups of neighbours, and since you are likely familiar with them, could you ascertain who is coming and if any of them are gentlemen I should avoid. I should hate to flirt with the wrong sort of gentleman."

"Unattached gentlemen, you say?"

"I thought I had heard Mrs. Cooper mention something about it to your aunt. I do not know if it is true or not, but I did not wish to ask as that would be rather forward and would make it seem as if I was too eager to meet gentlemen."

"And are you eager?"

"No, not really, but I thought it best to be prepared. I assure you that I will not ask this service of you often. In fact, if you would write your opinions on a paper and seal it, then I could see if my assessment matches yours after meeting these possible gentlemen. It would be an excellent way to evaluate my skill, would it not be?" She stopped walking and covered her hand that lay on his arm with her other hand. "No. No, that will not do. I will just tell you about whomever I meet when I see you next week, and then you can tell me if I have judged correctly. You do not even need to discover who might be invited to these parties. I shall tell you all when I see you."

His lips tipped up into a small smile that did not seem to hold much happiness. "You are intent upon preparing yourself, are you not?"

"A lady cannot rely on her friends forever. She must sooner or later learn to stand on her own, and I should like that to happen sooner rather than later." The thought was not an easy one to consider. It made her heart flutter with apprehension though a part of her mind also thought the idea a trifle exhilarating.

"I suppose you are correct," he replied. "I wish you success and look forward to hearing your report."

"You are leaving then?"

"I think it best."

She did not, but if he was determined to leave her then there was not much else to do than resign herself to it. "Then, let us make this a long walk, for I am in no hurry to be parted from such pleasure as your company."

Chapter 5

"Georgiana."

From the place where he sat near the window in his sitting room, Alfred could hear the scowl in Mr. Darcy's tone.

"What are you doing?"

"I was just going to see if I could do anything to ease Mr. Alfred Langley's plight."

Alfred straightened in his chair. She was?

Lorcan kicked his foot. "I think someone has an admirer," he hissed.

"I do not." Did he?

"By visiting him in his apartment?"

Mr. Darcy sounded even less pleased than before.

"I was going to knock and ask Mr. Langley – Mr. Lorcan Langley – if there was anything I could do. Kitty said he was with his cousin."

From the sounds of things, there were two displeased Darcys just outside Alfred's door.

"Go see what can be done to stop that argument before it begins," Alfred said to Lorcan.

"Knocking at a gentleman's private quarters is not proper."

"Fitzwilliam!"

The name was followed by what sounded like the stamp of a foot.

"How long will it be before you trust me? I am not a child any longer. I know what is proper and what is not."

"Please," Alfred begged Lorcan.

"Then, why are you here?"

"He seems so pleasant when with Kitty and his wife," Lorcan muttered.

"Mr. Darcy is more than her brother. He must also fill the role of parent. Now, please, put an end to it." Alfred tipped his head toward the door. "Or," he pushed up from his seat, "help me find the door." He swung his arm in front of him until it hit what felt like a human form, and from the "ouch" which accompanied the contact, he was certain he had found his cousin.

Thankfully, his cousin did not push him away, but instead, took him by the elbow and helped him cross the room and fully opened the door, which had been standing ajar so that the breeze might flow more easily through Alfred's sitting room.

"Oh, my!" he heard Georgiana gasp.

"She has seen you and is glaring at her brother," Lorcan whispered in Alfred's ear.

"Miss Darcy," Alfred said, "I would say it is a delight to see you, but that would not be entirely true today as my ability to see is less than ideal. However, it is a pleasure to hear you. Is there something I can do for you?"

"For me?" Georgiana cried. "I should think it would be dreadfully poor manners for me to come looking for assistance from a gentleman who was injured fetching me a flower to sketch."

"Do not apologize again."

"But if you had not tried to shoo that bee away from me..."

"I knew the risk." He had not, however, expected to get stung more than once and he would not have expected the stings to be near his eyes.

"I still feel dreadful."

"I assure you that I likely look worse than I feel, though, without the ability to open my eyes to use a looking glass, I cannot say for certain if that is true."

"I hope it is," Miss Darcy said, "for it looks very painful."

"I am happy to hear that your spirits seem uninjured," Mr. Darcy said.

"Mr. Darcy, I did not see you there." Alfred laughed at his own joke which, thankfully, seemed to lessen the formality he could feel in the air.

"I was wondering if I could do anything for you," Mr. Darcy said.

"You were?" Miss Darcy sounded excessively surprised.

"Yes, I was. I knew how distressed you were about Mr. Alfred Langley's injury, and I thought I might be able to alleviate some discomfort for both you and him."

"I will admit to being rather bored, and I was hoping to go spend some time in another room. Not that I can see the difference just yet, but there might be something of interest to listen to."

"You are not going downstairs, are you?" Lorcan asked.

"No, I know your mother will likely have callers, and I have no desire to be the ghastly, yet entertaining, topic of conversation." Once again, he laughed.

"I do not know how you can be so light-hearted while injured," Miss Darcy said.

"It is his nature to see the good in things rather than dwelling on the unpleasant," Lorcan explained. "According to my mother and his mother, of all us children, Alfred was the one who smiled the most as an infant."

"Could we go to the small sitting room with the window that overlooks the garden?" Alfred asked.

He would rather not stand around in the hallway discussing himself as a child when he could not see the reactions of those to whom the stories were being told. Did their eyes widen in surprise? Had either Darcy wrinkled their nose in amusement before politely smiling? Miss Darcy's nose wrinkled very prettily, and Alfred would not mind if she was amused. However, he would rather that her brother not laugh at him. It was bad enough that the gentleman seemed to look askance at him every time Alfred was in the vicinity of Miss Darcy.

"Would you like me to read to you?" Miss Darcy asked as they moved down the hall. "Or

Fitzwilliam can. He is a very good reader. I have always liked listening to him read to me."

Alfred had no great desire to be read to by Mr. Darcy. Of course, he also had no desire to have that gentleman scowl at him – even if he could not see it – simply because he preferred Miss Darcy to read to him rather than her brother.

"Listening to a poem or two might be nice." There. He had accepted the offer without stating anything which could earn him a scowl. "Was it now a book of poems you were reading yesterday?" he asked Miss Darcy.

" It was! I will go get it."

"I will understand if you prefer for my sister to read to you rather than me," Mr. Darcy said once Alfred could no longer hear the sound of scampering slippers. "To be honest, I would feel rather awkward reading to another gentleman."

"Did you not read to the colonel when he was first injured?" Lorcan asked.

"No, I did not. Wes insisted on providing that service until Lydia claimed it."

Lorcan chuckled. "Wes does enjoy performing."

"Indeed, he does," Darcy agreed with a chuckle of his own.

"We are here," Lorcan said to Alfred.

"I am sorry about your eyes," Mr. Darcy said. "I know that it could not have been prevented, but Georgiana often takes on things as if they are her responsibility even when they are not. It is a family trait, I fear."

There was a pause as Lorcan led Alfred to a chair. It was the blue one with the wings which Alfred preferred.

"I heard you had intended to travel home today," Mr. Darcy continued after Alfred was seated. "If you wished to do so before your eyes heal, you are welcome to use my carriage since riding your horse would be inadvisable at present."

"Thank you. I will consider it. Your sister does not seem to need my assistance any further and, frankly, I am unable to offer any in my current condition if she did."

He heard Mr. Darcy blow out a great breath.

"She does seem to be doing quite well. I think the shadow that has hung over her for the past two years is finally lifting for good."

A hand clasped Alfred's shoulder.

"Thank you for that."

Alfred nodded, not knowing exactly how else to

respond. Did this mean that the man would finally stop frowning at him? That was a hopeful thought.

"However, we still understand each other, do we not?"

Apparently, the frowning was to continue. "Indeed, we do."

"I will send her maid to sit with you if Georgiana has not already thought to see to that. Enjoy the poetry."

He heard Mr. Darcy leave at the same time that Lorcan dropped heavily into a chair near him.

"What did he mean by that last bit about understanding each other?" Lorcan asked.

"It is just a reminder that his sister is still not out."

"Did you talk to him about courting her?" Lorcan whispered.

"No, I talked to him about *not* courting her, and he seems unwilling to trust that I only wish to be her friend."

Lorcan laughed. "He's no fool."

"What does that mean?" Alfred asked.

"Ah, Miss Darcy, I see you have found your book. Would you be disappointed if I were to leave you to see to my cousin's entertainment while I find Kitty and send up a cold compress or a poultice for Alfred?"

"Oh, not at all. My maid is on her way."

"So, your brother said," Lorcan replied.

Georgiana sighed but said nothing until Lorcan was safely away. "He does not trust me."

"Lori?" Alfred asked though he knew of whom she spoke.

"No," she replied with a laugh. "My brother. I had hoped he would trust me by now. I have done everything I can to prove to him that I am not the silly girl I was in Ramsgate, and still, he does not trust me."

Alfred reached to his right where he knew she was sitting. After a bit of patting of the chair's arm, a soft hand grasped his. Why did he feel the need to hold her hand every time they spoke of delicate things? He should withdraw his hand. He should, but he was not going to. Hopefully, she would move her hand before her maid or anyone else – especially her brother – saw that they were holding hands.

"Are you certain he does not trust you?"

"Just earlier in the hall, he thought I was being improper coming to see if you needed anything."

"I know. I heard," Alfred admitted. "But I wonder if trust is the issue or if it is something else."

"What else could it be?"

After a minute of quiet contemplation, Alfred groaned. "Of course." He shook his head as Mr. Darcy's words to him in the hall while Georgiana was gone to retrieve her book repeated in his mind. "I would guess that the weight of responsibility for you and your safety hangs heavily on him. I reckon that while you consider what happened with Mr. Wickham to be your folly alone, he sees it as his."

"But it is not his fault. I have told him this many times." Frustration laced her words.

"And how many times have I told you that my swollen eyes are not your fault?"

"That is different."

He could hear the pretty scowl she wore in her words.

"No, it is not. You are both excessively good at caring for others. Perhaps, you are too good."

"That makes no sense." Her hand withdrew from his.

"Yes, it does," he pressed.

"You are very disagreeable, Mr. Langley."

"Only because I know I am right."

"Then explain to me how someone being too good at caring for others is a fault."

"Are you glaring at me?"

"Perhaps." Her reply was slow in coming.

"And are your arms folded?"

"They might be," she answered reluctantly.

He chuckled. "I did not mean to offend you or make you angry."

"I am not."

"Oh, I think you are."

She huffed but did not reply.

"Caring for others is a wonderful thing to do. However, such a caring lady, much like yourself, must not choose to wear responsibility that is not for her to wear. You asked me to pick a flower. I wished to grant you your request. Neither of us saw the bees at that time. My picking the flowers stirred them, and then when one buzzed near you, I thought only of saving you from being stung. I did not consider that in so doing I might anger more than that one bee by stepping off the path into where they had been feeding on the flowers. We made choices. Those choices ended in bee stings, including the ones which have made my eyes swollen. You are only responsible for your actions, not mine, and not those of the bees. And you did not come away from the encounter without a couple of stings yourself. Should I count them as my fault?"

Silently and patiently, he waited for her to respond.

"I see your meaning," she finally said. "You must think me a fool," she added quietly.

"Never." The word popped out of his mouth before it had even passed through is head. "I could never think of you as a fool, for fools do not care if they are foolish, and as I think I have already stated, you care a great deal. Now, might we have some poetry," he added as he heard someone, most likely her maid, enter the room.

"Of course." She opened her book. "You truly do not think of me as foolish?"

He shook his head. "I do not."

She paused, and he wondered what her face looked like in that quiet moment.

"I am glad," she said softly, with a touch of her hand to his. Then, she began reading, and Alfred rested his head against one of the wings of the chair and amused himself by imagining her expressions while listening to her sweet voice.

Chapter 6

My Dearest Aunt,

I am writing to you today from a new room as we have arrived at Winsdale Court. Our journey was not long — for as you know there are not many miles between Winsdale and Ravincot — nor was it eventful. Instead, it was as any good travel should be – dull enough to have a good conversation, read a book, and nod off for a nap.

Let me begin by telling you that the oddest thing happened just before our departure today. We had eaten breakfast and spent a little time in the garden since Kitty wished to do so, and I must admit, it was nice to have legs that welcomed a rest when we entered the carriage. But, I digress. As we were preparing to take our leave – even when we were standing in front of our carriage – Mr. C appeared to call on me!

You do remember Mr. C from my last page of writing,

do you not? I can now say that I not only suppose you would not approve of him but, with confidence, I can declare you would not. I must also say that his handsomeness fades in light of his forward actions. Upon arriving, he seemed relieved to see that we had not yet departed and wasted no time in dismounting from his horse and coming to my side.

Apparently, I troubled his mind from the moment he met me. Therefore, he had hurried to Ravincot because he wished to inform me, before I left the area, that he would be in town. And then, he did the most surprising thing by seeking permission to call on me at Darcy House! Fitzwilliam was relieved when I did not grant Mr. C the liberty he sought. I said it would be better to behave in town as we would have had we never met. There are yet many months before the season begins, and, since I have not yet officially entered society, it would be wrong for me to act as if I had. He was quite disappointed I can assure you! Unfortunately, I do not think he is dissuaded from his pursuit.

Fitzwilliam grumbled at some length for at least a quarter-hour once we had entered the carriage. As you may guess, he will not be welcoming Mr. C to Darcy House, and I, for one, am glad of it. Such gentlemen are enough to make a lady wish to retire to the country and *remain there even if it means being a spinster! But do not worry, my lady, I shall not be so easily defeated.*

I believe there was some good that came from such a strange encounter, for Fitzwilliam declared he was impressed with how well I handled the situation. Perhaps he will now begin to feel less anxious about my season much like I am beginning to believe I am more capable than I first supposed.

Georgiana paused and sat back to ponder that fact. She had met with three eligible gentlemen while at Ravincot. None of the three had been unbearable to look at or speak to. Mr. C — Mr. Clements — had been the most handsome. However, there was something about the way he had flattered and smiled which had unsettled her. It was far too reminiscent of Mr. Wickham. She had only hesitated in declaring him as an unfit candidate because she had not wished to condemn him for the faults of another.

This morning's unexpected call, however, had put that fear to rest. She was now discrediting him on his own behaviour alone. Whomever she chose to allow the privileged of calling on her would be a gentleman who held to propriety and approached her with care and a great deal less impertinent passion than either Mr. Wickham or Mr. Clements had done.

She turned back to her letter.

I am certain you will like Mr. Alfred Langley's mother. She is friendly but quiet – not excessively reserved, just not boisterous or in need of constant amusement. She has a personal library, which she has offered the use of to both Kitty and myself for the short time that we are here. It is housed in a pair of matching bookcases in the small drawing room behind her husband's study.

That room also has an easel which is always at the ready for her to paint since that is one of her favourite things to do. It stands just in front of garden doors that open onto the edge of the garden and the path which turns to the wildwood beyond. Trees are her favorite thing to paint. She does them both as they should appear in nature and as they might appear in a fairyland where colours do not stay where we mortals think they should. (That is just how she explained it.)

There is a lively intelligence to her eyes that renders her beautiful beyond her features, which are not to be described as lacking, but they are also not memorable. It is her eyes and smile which one remembers.

In comparing her to the Mrs. Langley we left at

Ravincot, this Mrs. Langley is more particular. She is kind, do not misunderstand me, but she more readily raises a displeased brow and expects things to be made right immediately. However, from what I have observed of her staff and her children, as well as her husband, she is adored. It is a peculiar balance of strictness and com-passion which she possesses. To be honest, Aunt, I can think of no better way to describe her to you than to tell you that her youngest son, and your soon-to-be new par-son, is much like her.

Before I forget. I am to impart to you her gratefulness for your husband's willingness to give a living to her son.

And with that, I think I have written enough for one day. I will leave my impressions of Winsdale, and its other inhabitants, for another time as I have yet to meet the youngest members of the Langley family.

Your loving niece, G.

~*~*~

"Did you get your letter written?" Ellen Langley asked from her place of repose when Georgiana arrived on the terrace. She motioned to the chair next to her in invitation. "The others are taking a walk, but my ankles will not survive a walk with so warm as it is today." She shifted her position and wiggled her toes. "I will be fortunate to be able to put my slippers back on when it is time to go in."

There was a squeal of delight somewhere to their left which drew Georgiana's attention before she sat down.

"What has my Lily so delighted?" Ellen asked.

There was a hedge which, if one was not standing as Georgiana was, obscured the view to the part of the garden in which Alfred and his brother, Edgar, were playing with Lily and Nathaniel.

"Her uncle has lifted her to his shoulders and is galloping down the lawn with Nathaniel giving chase." It was a delightful scene. Georgiana could have stood there for an hour watching Alfred run and play with his niece and nephew, but instead, she took a seat next to Ellen.

"Alfred will be such a good father," Ellen said. "Much like his brother is."

"It does appear as if you are correct."

"What do you think of our Alfred?"

Georgiana's eyes grew wide.

"Yes, I realize I am being very forward since we have just met. However, I feel as if I know you, for Alfred has spoken about you, your brother, and your friend a great deal." Ellen took a sip of the lemonade that was on the small table between them. "Would you care for some lemonade?" She asked. "I would pour for you but maneuvering around this large belly is challenging." She reached for the bell.

"I can pour it," Georgiana assured her. "There is no need to call a maid." She stood and, after a quick peek towards the garden where the children and Alfred were playing, filled a glass for herself.

"So?" Ellen asked upon the moment when Georgiana had regained her seat. "What do you think of Alfred?"

"He is a very kind gentleman." Hopefully, her companion would think her cheeks were rosy because of the warm weather. "We have become good friends in a very short time."

Ellen smiled. "Yes, I can see that."

"He will make an excellent parson," Georgiana said to fill the silence.

"He will," Ellen agreed before falling silent again.

"His eyes are looking much better." She should have written to her aunt about the estate instead of coming down to the garden just so she could see Alfred.

Ellen laughed. "Indeed, they are. He was quite a sight when he arrived. Lily cried when she saw him while Nathaniel scolded him for swatting at a bee."

Georgiana attempted to ignore the pang of guilt that sprung up unbidden.

"Did you draw the flower after?" Ellen asked.

"Yes," Georgiana replied with a nod. "I would feel much worse about his injury if I had not completed the drawing which inspired the whole incident." She took a sip of her lemonade. "It turned out well."

"If you will allow me to be forward once more, I would love to see it, as would Lily. She is particularly fond of flowers and that was one of the things she wished to know after she had dried her eyes. Her first question was if the lady Uncle helped was pretty, and then she wished to know if the pretty lady had drawn the flower."

Georgiana smiled at being called *the pretty lady*. "I would be happy to show it to her. It is in my desk in my room. Should I go get it now?"

"No, no. I would not send you running as that would leave me without a companion." She sighed. "I spend a great deal more time sitting and watching than I do participating these days. It gets to be very dull."

"Mr. Alfred Langley said that you were anxious to meet your baby."

"I am, and I would suggest that, should you have a choice once you are married, that you would refrain from being pregnant in the summer. It is much easier to sit beside a fire with one's feet up in the winter than it is to watch the pleasantness of summer pass one by."

"I... I... I shall keep that in mind," Georgiana stammered.

Ellen laughed. "Forgive me. I must remember that you only have a brother. Do you have any female cousins?"

"One."

"But you are not close, are you?"

"No, we are not. My closest cousins are Lord Westonbury and Colonel Fitzwilliam, who is my guardian along with my brother."

"Do you have many intimate friends?"

"I have a few, but Kitty is my dearest friend."

"She seems like such a sweet young lady – very much like the sort of lady whom I always imagined Lori would fall in love with." Ellen shifted again.

"May I impose upon you to help me to my feet. I do not wish to go walking, but I should like to see what my young ones are doing. I have not heard a peal of laughter in a full ten minutes. I wonder if their father has returned them to the nursery without a kiss for their mother."

Georgiana happily stood and offered her hand to help Ellen rise from her chair.

"Has Alfred told you that he played a part in my marrying his brother?"

"No, he has not." Curiosity rose within Georgiana. She could not imagine what role Alfred might have had in bringing his brother and Ellen together.

"There is a pond just beyond that stand of trees." Ellen pointed to their left. Beyond where her children were playing, there was a pretty little flower garden and just behind that was a stand of trees.

"It is a perfect place to take the children swimming," she continued. "Alfred and Edgar, as well as John their other brother, often use it for swimming. I did not know that the first time I came to visit Winsdale in the summer.

"It was a hot day in August, much like today. The sun was bright, the breeze was light, and the air was close. I decided to take a walk in the flower garden but when I grew warm, I sought the shade of the trees. Imagine my delight when I saw a pond and contemplated removing my stockings and dipping my feet in it." She chuckled. "Just as I reached the pond, Edgar was exiting it." She leaned close to Georgiana. "I do not wish to startle you too much, but he was not swimming with clothes on."

Georgiana gasped.

"I should have turned and walked away. However, I did not. I stood there in stunned silence, unable to move and with my feet rooted to the ground just as surely as the trees were rooted in place. Edgar quickly wrapped himself in a towel and attempted to apologize for his appearance. Then, he attempted to find his clothes, but they were missing. Alfred had hidden them. By the time Edgar had made this realization, I could both speak and move as the shock had worn off, but instead of leaving, as I knew I should, I chose to stay and help him look for his clothes. Well, I will not go into detail, but one thing led to another, and we ended up kissing. That is when my father found me."

"Oh, my."

"Indeed. There was nothing to do but marry."

She was looking wistfully in the direction of her husband. "It was the best mistake I have ever made." She rested a hand on the top of her swollen abdomen. "I loved him then, but not nearly so much as I do now." She turned to Georgiana with a smile. "It still surprises me how a poor decision on my part has become such a blessing." She waved to her husband, who said something to his son and the two of them started toward the terrace with Alfred and Lily following behind.

As Georgiana watched Alfred walking with Lily's hand in his, she wished with all her heart that her mistakes had been the sort that could be molded into a happy future, but they were not. They were the exact sort which would keep her from the future that, in this moment, she realized she desired more than any other. Courting Alfred was not just a pleasant idea or a means of escape or seeing her friend happy. He was perfectly suited to her. In the short time in which they had been acquainted, he had come to know and understand her so well. He guided her gently but never thought of her as foolish for needing advice. He approached her as if her presence and her thoughts were precious treasures to be sought with reverence. And yet, because of her mistakes, her errors in judgment, he would never be hers. She blinked against the tears that gathered.

"I will go get my flower drawing," she said to Ellen, and without looking at her companion, she fled toward the safety of her room.

Chapter 7

"Where is the pretty lady?" Lily asked as she and Alfred approached the terrace.

"Her name is Miss Darcy," Alfred corrected as he wondered the same thing. Georgiana had been with Ellen when he had started in this direction.

"Where is Miss Darcy?" Inquisitive, four-year-old eyes peered up at him.

"I am not sure where she is, Lily." He smiled at her frown and then tapped her nose. Doing so usually made her giggle, but not today. "You will get to meet her," he assured her. "You just must be patient." Which was easier said than done.

Lilly was not the only one who was anxious to see Miss Darcy. Alfred should not be so eager. He had spent the past five days telling himself he would not be any more delighted to see Georgiana than he was to see his cousin. However, it appeared he had done a dreadful job of listening to himself.

"She has gone to get a picture to show you," Ellen said with a smile for her daughter. "I told her how you wished to see the flower she drew."

Ah, that was where she was. He would not have to wait too much longer to see her. Alfred had greeted her when she arrived, but it had only been a brief welcome, nothing more.

"Come and sit in the shade for a while," Lily's mother continued.

"Is it a picture of the flower that Uncle took from the bee?" Lily climbed up on a chair at the table which was laid out with a light lunch.

"Be careful with this. You do not wish to have to change your dress before you meet Miss Darcy," her father cautioned as he handed her a glass of lemonade.

"I did not take the flower from the bee," Alfred said.

Lily's head bobbed up and down. "Yes, you did. That is why it hurt you."

"That is not why the bee stung him," Nathaniel argued. "Uncle swatted at the bee, and one should never do that."

Alfred shook his head and chuckled. "You look very much like your father when you scowl like that, Nate."

The comment caused his seven-year-old nephew to beam with pleasure. The boy wanted nothing more at the moment than to be like his father. It was not a terrible goal to which to aspire. Alfred could remember a time when he felt the same about his own father and nearly the same about his eldest brother, Edgar.

"You must remember that I only did it to protect Miss Darcy. I did not wish for her to be injured."

"And did it work?" Nate's left eyebrow arched. He really was a lot like his father.

"Until I stepped off the path and angered the other bees, yes, it worked. After that, Miss Darcy did end up with a few stings but not so many as I did."

"I think we have heard enough about that incident," Edgar inserted as he sat down next to his wife. "Your uncle promises to be more careful around bees." His eyes were filled with humor for he enjoyed seeing someone besides himself scolding his youngest brother. "I see you have abandoned your slippers again, my dear," he said to his wife. "My bill for stockings is going to be quite large before this child arrives."

Ellen batted her lashes. "I could go without them."

Edgar's eyes narrowed but his lips remained tipped in an amused smile. "Is that what you wish to teach our daughter?"

"I would love for her to learn that she may go without stockings if she is pregnant and her husband does not find it offensive."

Edgar laughed. "I do not find it offensive, but there is more than me about whom to think. I am certain our guests would find it unusual, to be polite about it."

"Other than not wishing to wear your shoes, are you well?" Alfred asked with a glance toward the door to the terrace.

"Yes, I am well," Ellen assured him.

"And Miss Darcy?" Edgar asked with a smirk for his brother. "Is she also well?"

Ellen's brow furrowed.

Was something wrong with Georgiana?

"I believe she is."

"But you are uncertain?" Her husband's smirk faded.

Ellen shrugged. "She left me rather quickly." She smiled at her children who were watching her with no little amount of interest. "I am certain she is well. Travelling is tiring. Remember how you both fall asleep whenever we visit Aunt Meri?"

Alfred hoped that was all it was, but he had his doubts. If the children were not present, he would have asked Ellen what she and Georgiana had been discussing before Georgiana had scurried away. However, there was no need to worry the children – especially Lily who had been most anxious all day to meet her uncle's pretty new friend.

"Ah, here are my little darlings," Alfred's mother said as she and those who had been strolling in the garden joined them. "Did you have fun playing?"

Both Nathaniel and Lily assured their grand-mother that they had.

His mother's eyes looked around the gathered group. "We seem to be missing one. Is Miss Darcy still composing her letter?"

"I thought I had seen her exit the house," Mr. Darcy added.

"She is gone to get a picture," Ellen said.

"Of a flower – the one Uncle Alfred took from the bee," Lily added.

"I did not take it from the bee," Alfred retorted.

"She wants to show it to me," Lily continued, completely ignoring her uncle's protest.

"That is a lovely thing to want to do," Alfred's mother said to Lily before turning her attention to her guests. "You have a very thoughtful sister, Mr. Darcy. You have done well by her."

The man smiled and accepted the compliment graciously while adding his own commendations about his sister.

It was another five minutes, at least, before Georgiana joined them. She smiled sweetly and blushed as she made her excuses for being tardy.

"There was no specified time," Mrs. Langley said. "I understand you were on a mission to retrieve something that my granddaughter would dearly love to see." She looked at Alfred. "Would you like to introduce your friend to your niece and nephew?"

Mr. Darcy's left brow did that critical arching thing that it liked to do, but, fortunately, it was not accompanied by a scowl.

"If you wish, I will."

"I do," his mother assured him.

"Miss Darcy, I would like you to meet two of my

favourite people in the whole world. This young man on my left is Master Nathaniel Langley and, on my right, is Miss Lily Langley. Nate, Lily, this is Miss Darcy." He turned to Nathaniel. "She is Mr. Darcy's little sister."

"Like me!" Lily's legs were swinging back and forth as they hung over the edge of her chair, causing her to bounce where she sat.

"Yes, just like you," Alfred assured her. Then, he took a chair from the far side of Nathaniel and placed it near Lily. "Miss Darcy," he offered.

She hesitated.

"Lily is eager to see your drawing," he added. Why was she hesitating? Did she not wish to be near him? Or was it that she was not comfortable with children?

"Are you?" She smiled at Lily, who nodded.

That seemed to say that it was not discomfort with children which was causing her to hesitate. That thought only confused Alfred more. Why would she not wish to be near him?

"I have it in this book with several other flowers, but I think you will know which one it is." She sat down next to Lily and, opening her sketchbook, began paging through it.

"Oooh," Lily cooed, "they are very pretty."

"Thank you. I like drawing flowers."

"Grandmama likes drawing trees."

"Yes, she does. She told me that."

"Miss Darcy," Nathaniel interjected.

"Yes, Master Langley?"

"I am sorry you got stung."

"Thank you." She gave Alfred a curious look.

"I told them," he said softly. "It was part of the story about my eyes."

She nodded and continued turning pages.

"Did it hurt a lot?" Nathaniel asked.

"No more than one might imagine," she replied. "And likely not so much as your uncle's stings did."

"Oh, I see it!" Lily cried. "There is a bee on it!" She grabbed Alfred's arm. "See, Uncle Alfred, she gave the flower back to the bee."

"Indeed, she has. May I?" He asked with an outstretched hand.

"Of course." Georgiana placed the book in his hand.

"I thought it might be easier for Nathaniel to see this way," he explained.

"That is a very good thought."

Nathaniel scrutinized the picture for several

minutes, turning the book one way and then the other.

"It is very good," he finally said before giving the book back to Alfred, who allowed Lily a moment to look at the picture before returning it to Georgiana.

"May I see it?" Ellen asked.

"Miss Darcy will not get a chance to eat if we keep her so busy," Alfred's mother said as the book was being passed from Edgar on Georgiana's right to his wife. She nodded to Alfred that he should see that Miss Darcy be offered the plate of sandwiches and sweets.

He stood and moved the tiered plated down to where Georgiana could make her selections. "Would you like some lemonade or a cup of tea?"

"Oh, I had a glass of lemonade earlier." She looked behind her to where she and Ellen had been standing when he saw her while he was playing with the children.

"Allow me," he said before retrieving her glass from the table near the chairs behind the hedge.

Then, with frustration building inside of him, he sat back down. He was happy to see her, but this stilted polite conversation was not for what he wished. He wanted to know everything which had happened at Ravincot in his absence. Most especially, he wanted to hear about the dinner parties she had attended. However, he could not ask her about that here, and he was not certain when he would get the opportunity to speak to her in private.

"I understand you have another sister who is marrying soon," his mother was saying to Kitty.

"That is correct. Lydia and the colonel will be married at the end of the month," Kitty replied.

"And she is the youngest? Is that correct?"

"Yes."

"Five daughters," his mother said with awe. "That must have been a very active household in which to grow up. I know our home was never without some bit of excitement with our three boys, was it, dear?"

"No, it was never dull," Alfred's father said. "However, it was never topsy-turvy either." He smiled broadly. "My boys are not so boisterous as some. The older two were more of a challenge than Alfred, however."

"Yes, if we had all been as amiable as Alfred, there might be more of us," Edgar said with a laugh. "However, he was just as capable of causing a stir as any of us were." He tilted his head and raised a brow at Alfred. "Neither John nor I ever caused so large a disturbance as Alfred did one summer at the pond."

Alfred covered his heart with his hand and affected an affronted look. "Me? I only hid your clothes. The rest of the disturbance, as you call it, was all your doing, Brother."

Alfred's dad chuckled. "And it all worked out for the best, did it not?"

"Yes, it did."

"Which means," Alfred inserted with a grin, "that even when starting trouble, I do so to the benefit of others."

This, of course, led to all of his family laughing and the story of how Ellen and Edgar came to be married was shared – in terms which were appropriate for the ears of children while still allowing the adults to understand what had happened.

Nearly everyone enjoyed the story – even Mr. Darcy chuckled at it. However, there was one person who seemed not to enjoy it. Georgiana smiled while listening, but it was not a smile of enjoyment. It was more an expression of politeness, and try as he might to engage her, she did not once look in Alfred's direction unless he was speaking to her. Something was not right. His hand fairly itched to hold hers and beg her to tell him what was troubling her.

Lily wrapped her arm around his and rested her head against him, drawing Georgiana's attention, and that was when he saw it. She was not merely troubled. There was sadness in her eyes. His heart clenched at the sight, and a desire to do bodily harm to whoever had caused such sorrow nearly overwhelmed him. She turned away, and a scowl settled on Alfred's face before he could stop it.

Edgar's eyebrows rose in question when he glanced at Alfred, who shook his head and attempted to smile. No wonder Mr. Darcy scowled so often as he did when someone with the potential to do his sister harm came near her. It was just what one did when one loved someone so dearly.

Good heavens! Alfred gasped as a shocking realization washed over him.

Gasping, however, was a very poor thing to do when eating a sandwich, for breathing became an impossibility when a piece of food lodged itself in one's windpipe. Alfred attempted to cough but could not.

Thankfully, Nathaniel noticed his uncle's distress, and, after a fair bit of smacking on the back by Nathaniel and Edgar, followed by a well-placed punch to the gut, Alfred was once again able to draw a breath as he coughed the bit of food out of the way and swallowed it properly with a bit of lemonade.

He loved Georgiana Darcy.

And he had no idea what he was going to do about it.

Falling in love had not been part of his plan. He was to settle into his position as a parson, and then, in a year or two, he was going to begin looking for a wife. However, in a year or two, Georgiana might be married to someone else.

He cast a look in Mr. Darcy's direction. He had time to figure it out. Georgiana was not yet out, and there was no way, absolutely none, that Alfred was going to even suggest that he be allowed to court her until it was proper to do so.

Chapter 8

"Are you well?" Fitzwilliam sat down next to his sister in the drawing room at Winsdale. They had finished dinner a short time ago, and the gentlemen had just rejoined the ladies.

Georgiana closed the book she was not reading. "I am tired. I would like to retire early, but I confess that I am worried it will offend Mrs. Langley." And that worry was only slightly stronger than the one about how to act around Alfred.

She had managed to deflect much of his attention this afternoon by offering to draw a flower just for Lily – one that the little girl chose.

As it turned out, picking just the right flower was no easy task for a four-year-old. They must have examined every flower in Winsdale's garden before Lily decided upon a rose that had not yet opened because it reminded her of her baby sister or brother. Alfred had been right about his niece being excited for her mother's baby to be born, for it was difficult to have a conversation of any great length with Lily without hearing about how she was going to be a big sister.

Listening to a talkative child, coupled with keeping up the appearance of being nearly so enthralled as Lily was with all the flowers had been a tiresome task at times. However, it had kept Lily's uncle from asking Georgiana to take a walk in the garden with him.

"I am certain she would understand. You have had a long day," Fitzwilliam covered one of her hands with his.

She had always enjoyed when he did that – until tonight when it reminded her of how someone else also often did that. She wrapped her hand around her brother's fingers and gave them a squeeze as she attempted to ignore the pang of longing for Alfred's comfort. What would it be like to be able to rest her weary head against Alfred's shoulder as she had often done with both her father and brother, as well as Richard, over the years?

"Are you certain you are only tired?"

Georgiana nodded. "You know how I can become morose when weary."

Her cheeks began to feel warm. She did not like keeping things from her brother, especially when it was about a gentleman. She had kept her thoughts about such things from him at Ramsgate, and it had nearly turned to ruin.

Her brother's brow furrowed. "And to what have your morose thoughts turned?"

Drat! She had hoped he would just allow her to be tired. "It is nothing."

"I suspect you are not being honest with me," he said in that soft tone that spoke of his disappointment.

Immediately, tears sprang to her eyes. "Please, Fitzwilliam, can we just not speak of it here? I was only thinking about the season."

He grasped her hand more firmly and rose, pulling her to her feet with him. Then, he led her over to where Mrs. Langley was discussing weddings with Kitty, Elizabeth, and Ellen.

"If you will excuse us, I should like to see my sister to her room."

"Is she unwell?" Mrs. Langley's voice and expression were filled with concern.

"She has a bit of a headache. It is nothing severe."

"You will let me know if it grows worse, will you not?" She looked at Georgiana.

"Of course."

"We have powders should you need them."

Georgiana thanked her and allowed herself to be led from the room. "I do not have a headache, Fitzwilliam," she whispered when they had reached the corridor.

"Perhaps not now, but you always have one after crying."

"I am not crying."

"You are on the verge of tears. It is only a matter of time." He smiled gently at her. "Now, tell me what has you concerned about the season." They began the short climb up the stairs that led from the first floor to the second.

There was very little chance she was going to be able to avoid telling him what was on her heart. It was best to just tell him all now rather than some now and a bit later. Unless... "A gentleman of worth would be an honest man, would he not be?"

"Yes," Fitzwilliam answered simply, much to Georgiana's frustration. She had rather hoped he would begin a lecture on the dangers of disguise. However, it appeared she was not going to find a reprieve in that way.

"And he would wish for an honest wife, would he not?"

"That seems reasonable, but I do not know why that has you concerned."

"What if he discovers I have been deceitful?"

Darcy stopped walking. They had reached the landing and had moved three steps down the hallway. "What have you done?"

"Nothing!" Georgiana cried. "Well, not recently, that is, but you have not forgotten Ramsgate, have you?"

"How would anyone know about that?" Darcy demanded. "You are not going to tell them, are you?"

"N...o..." She huffed in exasperation. "Although if it is something I conceal until I am married, and then it is discovered, will that not be worse?"

"I think a gentleman of worth would understand." There was a firm set to his jaw that gave lie to his words.

"And you would be understanding if you discovered that Elizabeth nearly eloped with a gentleman years before she met you and did not tell you about it because she was afraid you would not wish to offer for her if you knew?"

"Elizabeth did not..."

"But she could have. Pretend, Fitzwilliam." She pulled him by his sleeve towards her room. "What if it had happened?" Could he not see how her stupidity when she was younger had put her in a difficult situation now? To tell of her folly to the wrong person might leave her with a tainted reputation, but not to tell of her folly to the right person, might cause him to resent marrying her later.

"I would not be happy," he finally admitted after they had tromped down the length of the hallway. "However, I love her, and we would find a solution. You just need to find a gentleman who loves you as dearly as I love Elizabeth and whom you love just as dearly in return."

"But I could love someone, and it could be the one thing that keeps me from him."

True to her brother's words, it had not taken long for her to dissolve into tears. It only took the thought of her foolishness keeping her from Alfred to turn her into a watering pot. Her shoulders shook as she took shuddering breaths while the sorrow of such a thought, which she had pushed aside since her realization in the garden earlier, fully engulfed her and spilled down her cheeks.

The door beside her was thrown open, and she was pulled inside and then into her brother's embrace as soon as the door was closed.

"You are not that girl any longer," he whispered against her hair as he rubbed her back. "Any man who loves you will understand that. He has likely done things in his past which were not wise."

She shook her head. "What if he discovers it before he has the chance to love me?"

The soothing circles on her back ceased. "Are we still speaking of what could be or what has happened?" There was a hint of a hard edge to his words.

"Must I tell you?"

"It is Langley," he growled. "You should not have told him."

Georgiana pulled away from her brother. "How do you know that I told him about Ramsgate?"

Fitzwilliam's eyes grew wide and then he closed them, squeezing them tightly shut. "He told me."

"He what?"

"He told me that you had told him about Ramsgate."

"Why would he tell you that?" He had said he would not tell anyone. Anyone! She had trusted him.

"I might have approached him at Ravincot about his intentions regarding you."

Georgiana wiped at her damp cheeks with the palm of her hand. "Might have or did, Fitzwilliam? Which is it?"

Pulling his handkerchief out of his pocket, he handed it to her. "Did."

"What reason could you possibly have for doing that?"

"He was at Ravincot, waiting for you."

"Because he is my friend and wished to make me feel at ease."

"I know. That is what he told me. He also assured me that he would never do anything to harm you." His eyes narrowed. "Has he done this," he waved a hand at her, "knowingly?"

Her eyes grew wide. "What?"

"Does he know how you feel about him? Has he played with your heart?"

"No, no, he would never do that, Fitzwilliam."

She grasped his forearms which were folded across his chest. "Mr. Alfred Langley is all that is good. In fact, I knew from the beginning of our friendship that he was too good for me." She shrugged. "Yet, I fell in love with him anyway." Again, the tears began to fall.

Fitzwilliam's head snapped back, and he shook it as if clearing his mind after being hit. "Too good for you? Did he tell you that?"

Was her brother looking for a reason to be angry with Mr. Langley? "No. He did not tell me that. Or, at least, he did not in those words."

She dried her face with one hand while keeping her other hand on her brother's arm. She knew she would not be able to stop him if he decided to storm out of the room, but she hoped that her touch would keep him reasonable.

"I am going to need an explanation," his voice was gruff.

"Perhaps you should sit down."

He gave her a wary look but took a seat in the rocking chair near the window since the other chair in that grouping held her sketchbook.

"Explain," he said as soon as he was seated.

"It all began with a promise." She told him how

Kitty had promised to stand with her during the season and how that promise had been the cause of so much heartache.

"I felt dreadful when I discovered that she had refused Mr. Lorcan Langley on my account."

Fitzwilliam was not looking pleased, and she suspected he wished to say something to her but was refraining. She drew a deep breath and released it.

"I wished to make things right, but I did not go about it in the right way." She pulled her lower lip between her teeth and grimaced.

He closed his eyes. "What did you do?"

"I asked Mr. Alfred Langley to pretend to court me."

"You did what?" her brother fairly bellowed.

"If Kitty thought I had found a trustworthy gentleman to court, she would then be released from her promise and could marry whenever she wished."

"You wished to perpetuate a lie to help your friend?"

"You do not need to scold me." She folded her arms and scowled at him. "Mr. Alfred Langley did a very good job of that when he refused my proposal."

"Well, he has sense. I will give him that."

"Do you wish for me to tell you or not?" Tears were threatening again. She hated when her brother glowered at her as he was doing now.

"Forgive me. Please continue."

"As soon as you stop scowling at me." She held his gaze until he shook his head and a small smile touched his lips for a moment.

"You are stubborn," he muttered.

"As are you," she retorted.

"True. Now, please go on. I will do my best not to scowl, though I make no promises."

"It is a very fearsome expression."

"I apologize." He reached across the gap between them and gave her knee a pat.

"You are forgiven." Again, she drew a deep breath and willed herself to tell the rest without too many tears. "Mr. Alfred Langley told me that he could not be part of such a deception. So, I offered to allow him to court me in earnest."

Her brother's face scrunched as if keeping silent was painful.

"He told me that he needed a wife who was honest," she looked down at her hands which were clasped in her lap. How she wished that she was that honest lady he wanted for his wife. "Then, he asked why I was so fearful of the season, and that led to my telling him about Ramsgate." She lifted her eyes to her brother. "I thought about not telling him. I truly did consider it." Her shoulders sagged. "However, he seemed trustworthy, and I was so tired of being held back by my secret." She shook her head. "But I am. I still am, and I always shall be. I shall never be free of Wickham."

Chapter 9

"Why are you in this room rather than with everyone else in the garden?" Lorcan slipped into a chair next to his cousin in the library.

"I thought I would do some reading. It is not so very long until I take up my living." Alfred closed the book he held but kept his finger between the pages he had been attempting to read. "In fact, it might be best if I were to stay home tomorrow. Lord Matlock is expecting to install a parson well-versed in his knowledge of all things parson-like." He grinned at his cousin, hoping that such a comment accompanied by a smile might elicit a chuckle, which it did.

"I highly doubt that Lord Matlock expects you to know everything."

"Still. I think it is best if I remain behind and apply myself to my studies."

Staying home, much like hiding in this room, would make it a great deal easier to keep his desire to be more than Georgiana's friend a secret. Ever since he had come to the realization that he loved her, he had been able to see his interactions with her from a different perspective. He no longer wondered at Mr. Darcy's scowling at him so often. And if his actions when he had been unaware of his feelings for Georgiana had been so transparent as to anger her brother, how was he to hide his true feelings when he understood them?

"Books can be packed, and reading can be done anywhere."

"True," Alfred drew the word out as if he was not completely agreeing, "but it is much more peaceful here."

Something very heavy fell overhead.

"Yes," Lorcan said with a smirk, "so much more peaceful."

"It will be once everyone leaves," he argued just as the door opened, and Lily stepped inside.

"Uncle, Papa said we can play in the garden, are you coming?" Lily clasped her hands in front of her and waited hopefully. "Please," she added sweetly

"You know Edgar and his brood will still be here

even when everyone else leaves, do you not, Uncle?" Lorcan whispered.

Alfred shot his cousin a look of displeasure before answering Lily. "I will be right there."

The answer brought a smile of pure delight to the youngster's face. "I will wait."

"Are you alone?"

She nodded.

"Where is your nurse or your father?" How was he to prolong his departure from his hiding place if she was waiting for him?

"Papa is with Grandpapa and cannot be disturbed, and Helen is already in the garden with Nathaniel."

"Do either your father or nurse know you are here in the library?"

She nodded. "Grandmama said I should find you."

"Grandmama did, did she?" Of course, his mother would send Lily to fetch him. She knew that it was nearly impossible for him to say no to one of Lily's requests.

"Yes. Are you ready yet?"

"I do not see how I can be ready if I have been talking to you," Alfred replied in a teasing tone.

Lily huffed. "Then, stop talking to me."

Lorcan laughed. "She has a point."

"I suppose she does," Alfred admitted, opening his book once again so that he could pretend to read a few words before he put the book aside and joined Lily in the garden.

"Mr. Lori?"

"Yes, Miss Lily?"

"Will you play with me in the garden, too? Papa had the wickets placed."

"He will likely wish to walk with Miss Bennet," Alfred replied.

"Unless, she wishes to play croquet with Miss Lily," Lorcan retorted.

"I can ask her!" Lily cried. Then, she turned her attention back to Alfred. "Are you ready, yet, Uncle?" There was a distinct note of excited impatience to her tone.

Alfred clicked his book closed. "Yes, I am ready."

Lily skipped across the room and took his hand. "We should not dwawdle."

"Dawdle," Alfred corrected as he allowed her to lead him from the room.

"Yes," Lorcan muttered behind him, "so much more peaceful."

~*~*~

"You are correct," Alfred said to Lorcan some thirty minutes later while Georgiana and Miss Bennet strolled along the edge of the lawn and Lily chased her ball through the croquet field. "Netherfield's library might be quieter. However, who would hold Lily's baby while she played if I am not here?"

Lorcan laughed. "She has you completely in her pocket, does she not?"

"Completely," Alfred agreed. Lily could ask him to do just about anything – such as sit properly on a blanket and hold her doll so that it would not feel lonely while she played with her brother – and he would do it.

"I cannot blame you for it," Lorcan said. "She is a sweet young lady, is she not?"

Alfred nodded. "She must get it from her mother."

"I assume you are discussing my daughter," Edgar said as he took a seat next to Lorcan.

"Indeed, we are," Lorcan replied.

"And what is it that she gets from her mother?" He asked with a smile. "Besides her beauty, that is."

"Her sweet temperament," Alfred answered.

"What! You do not think I am sweet?" Edgar affected a look of indignation.

"No, I do not. I remember all too well how you and John used to tease and torment me."

Edgar laughed. "You were fun because, for a time, you would believe whatever we said, and John and I were young and stupid." He leaned back and propped himself up with his hands. "And I think that you fully repaid me for my tormenting when you hid my clothes that summer."

Alfred shook his head. "I am not so certain we are even. You ended up with a pretty and sweet wife as the result of my tormenting you, while I never remember you and John teasing me into anything pleasant." There had been scraped knees, a sore stomach, or switched britches at the end of many of his brothers' tauntings, but never had there ever been anything that did not involve some sort of discomfort for him waiting as a reward for doing whatever it was that his brothers had tricked him into doing.

"I could repay you properly for your service," Edgar said in a hushed tone. "Miss Darcy is both sweet and pretty, and from what I can see, you would not be opposed to being leg-shackled to her."

"No." Alfred's heart quickened its pace.

"That was a rather quick and harsh reply, do you not think, Lori?" Edgar asked with a laugh.

"Indeed, it was."

"Do you wish for her brother to kill me?"

Edgar laughed again. "I have noticed how he glares at you."

"Does he?" Lorcan asked.

"If you would take your eyes off of Miss Bennet for a few seconds, you would know," Edgar returned. "That was my first clue that my little brother was in love. Well, that and how he was so eager to tell Lily all about the pretty lady he had left behind at Aunt Meri's."

"She asked me about her. What was I supposed to do? Not answer?" Alfred snapped.

"Relax, Al. I am not going to compromise your lady." An eyebrow arched over one eye. "Unless, of course, it becomes necessary."

"She is not out yet, and we are just friends."

"Do you believe him?" Edgar asked Lorcan, who shook his head.

"Not once in all the times he has said it."

Alfred turned to face both his brother and his cousin. "Listen carefully. She is not out yet. I am not yet established in my profession. And we are just friends for that is all we can be."

Edgar leaned forward eagerly. "But you would like it to be more?"

"I did not say that," Alfred protested.

"But would you?"

"She is not out yet, I am not yet established in my profession, and we are just friends," Alfred repeated.

"I will take that as a yes. How about you, Lori?"

"I would agree. He is more than a little smitten."

"I have given my word to her brother that we are just friends," Alfred hissed the words through clenched teeth. "Now, leave off." Why must his brother and cousin be so annoying? "Here." He shoved the doll he held in his brother's direction. "Make sure she does not get too much sun and that the ants do not climb on her because they tickle."

Edgar laughed as he took the doll. "Yes, ma'am."

"I am only repeating what your daughter told me." Alfred pushed up from where he was sitting and placed his hat on his head.

"Wait. Where are you going?" Edgar asked. "We promise to stop teasing."

Alfred turned a look on his brother that said he very much doubted that was possible. "I am going to take a walk or perhaps a ride or some such thing that is far away from you," he glanced toward the edge of the lawn, "and her," he added in a low hiss before stalking away.

"It would be a fine day for a swim," his brother called after him.

"Shut up, Edgar," Alfred called back.

"Uncle Alfred!" Nathaniel, who had just hit his ball through the wicket closest to where Alfred was walking, cried in surprise.

"Forgive my language, Nate, but your father is being an arse." He stopped for a moment. "And you are only allowed to say such things when you are fully grown and your brother is teasing you relentlessly."

Nathaniel folded his arms across his chest. "Grandmama would not like it."

"Nor would your mother," Alfred agreed. "I shall apologize to them later." The child did not look convinced that such an answer was acceptable, but at present, that was the only answer

Alfred was prepared to give. "Your sister is waiting for you." And if Nathaniel did not return to the game soon, Lily would be at Alfred's side asking why he was grumpy.

At least, Nathaniel did not ask such pointed questions as his sister did. He only scolded without a care for why someone might be put out or behaving badly, which Alfred knew he was doing. His behavior was far from exemplary at present and it was most certainly that way because he was put out and bothered.

Reluctantly, his nephew turned back to the game he and his sister were playing.

"I will be back for dinner," Alfred said when Nathaniel cast a glance over his shoulder at him. If he planned it just right, he might be able to be back in time to have his dinner brought to his room rather than having to endure a meal seated with everyone and having them watch him.

He picked up a branch from under one of the trees when he reached the grove. There had been a good bit of wind three days ago and a few small limbs lay scattered on the ground. Thankfully, this one was long enough to thwack the weeds, which grew here and there, in a satisfying fashion. He would walk to the grotto and stay there until it was nearly time to dress for dinner. Then, he would make his way back. If he was fortunate, there might be some raspberries he could eat between now and then since he was going to miss having a cup of tea and some sweets on the terrace, which was not nearly so disappointing as not being able to sit with and speak to his charming and beautiful friend.

He shook his head and laughed at himself. How he had ever convinced himself that she was only his friend was a bit difficult to comprehend. He had found her enticing from the first day he had met her at Lord and Lady Matlock's house in town. She had so kindly offered her input when Lady Matlock was torturing Lorcan with pointed questions.

He stopped walking and turned to look back in the direction he had come.

Georgiana Darcy had the kindest and gentlest heart of anyone he had ever met. Was that not one reason why she had proposed her plan for him to court her? She had hoped to help keep a friend from suffering any inconvenience on her account.

He continued on his way toward the grotto.

Then, there was the other reason why she had proposed her plan, and it, too, spoke to the tenderness of her heart. For, what other sort of heart could be worked on so easily by a scoundrel? Even now as he thought about the tale she had told him, Alfred found himself growing angry at the perfidy of Mr. Wickham while his heart ached for the fear that such treatment had caused in one so kind and gentle as Georgiana. He could not, and he would not, allow her heart to be so damaged again.

The grotto stood before him, a pile of rocks covered with vines carefully arranged to appear as if it had always been there, though it was only a few years older than Alfred. Facing him, was the dining cavern. At least twice during the summer when he was a child, his mother would instruct the gardener to see that a table and chairs were placed at the grotto so that she could have a picnic there. There was a bench along the far wall of the cavern, but that was not where he was going to take his ease. He moved to the left and picked his way along the narrow stone path that circled the grotto. Built into the sides of the hill were sitting areas. One for each of his brothers and himself, as well as one for his mother and father.

The one next to his mother's and father's bench was his, and that is where he sat down, tucking himself into the corner and lifting his feet to rest on the opposite end of the bench. He sighed as the warm welcome of the grotto wrapped around him, making him feel secure. This, he thought, this was how he wished Georgiana's heart to feel – protected, welcomed, and at peace.

He closed his eyes and rested his head against a stone. There was, of course, only one way to ensure that he could see her cared for in such a way for all her life. He would just have to marry her. His lips tipped upward at the thought before his face pinched in a grimace that he rubbed at with his hands. He only needed to keep his desires in check for a while longer. The assembly in Meryton was just two months away. That was to be Georgiana's first foray into society as a debutante. After that, he would talk to her brother about being allowed to be more than Georgiana's friend.

He shook his head and sent a silent prayer heavenward that he would be able to survive two months of unspoken desires and that, at the end of that time, his request would be met with success. Of course, *not* travelling to Netherfield tomorrow would most certainly help with part of that.

Chapter 10

"Oh, it is lovely!" Kitty said as the Darcy carriage drove through the gate and toward the house at Beaumont Park the next afternoon. "Lydia must be delighted to know this will be her home."

"And you will not be so very far from her," Georgiana placed an arm around her friend and leaned against Kitty so she could also peer out the window. "I have not been here in some time."

"It has been at least five years," Fitzwilliam agreed. "However, I do think we will be stopping here more often on our way to and from Pemberley in the future since someone will be living here. I see the work on the chimney Richard told me about has begun."

"Are there many improvements to be made?" Elizabeth asked.

"No, just a few. I suspect they will be done before

Christmas since my uncle insisted that they were started just as soon as he knew that Richard was not going to be returning to his duty in the army."

"Lydia has chosen some paint and fabrics for a few of the rooms," Kitty added. "She told me about it in her last letter."

"I suppose she will want it all redone," Elizabeth said as she studied the house they were approaching. "I know how she has always dreamed of the day she could decorate her own home."

"I thought so, too," Kitty admitted. "However, she is only redecorating one drawing room and the master and mistress chambers. She said the rest is to her taste enough that it does not require an outlay of money."

"Indeed?" Elizabeth said in surprise.

"That is exactly how she put it," Kitty assured her sister. "Of course, she added that, so long as she has her colonel, the pattern of the paper in the dining room does not matter."

Elizabeth laughed. "Then, it seems she will be having the dining room redone next."

"Most likely," Kitty replied with a grin. "Although I do think she has changed enough to be patient and consider her projects carefully."

"I am certain you are correct," Elizabeth agreed.

"A lady should put her mark on her home," Fitzwilliam said.

"But not to the harm of her husband's accounts," Elizabeth countered.

"That is true. You know you can make more changes in town and at Pemberley."

"There are none that need to be made beyond the few changes to my bedchambers. Your mother had excellent taste."

"Someday, it will be us," Kitty said with a squeeze for Georgiana's hand.

"It will be very soon for you," Georgiana assured her friend. "You should be settled into your apartments at Ravincot well before a year from now is complete." Georgiana's hope of Kitty and Mr. Langley marrying any sooner than the end of the season had faded to nothing with her realization that she loved Alfred and would never be free of her folly in Ramsgate.

Kitty sat back as the carriage rolled to a stop. "About that," she began while they waited to have the door opened and the steps installed. "Lorcan and I decided last night that we will marry in June no matter what happens during the season."

Georgiana pulled her bottom lip between her teeth. "Are you certain?"

Kitty nodded. "We are both perfectly content. However, we are not making any announcement about it until after Lydia's wedding. She deserves her time to be the center of attention. I would not wish to take anything away from her."

"Oh, of course," Georgiana agreed.

"However, Lorcan and I wished for you to know our plans so that you do not feel as if you are impeding them." Her brows rose and her lips pursed as she gave Georgiana a pointed look.

"I cannot help feeling as if I am," Georgiana muttered.

"That is because you are a Darcy," Fitzwilliam said. "We tend to feel the weight of responsibility far more than we likely should." His smile was gentle and reassuring.

"Yes, but," she said as he exited the carriage, "in this case, I am not taking on a responsibility which is not mine."

"Yes, you are," Kitty argued. "*I* made the promise. You did not ask me to make it." She blew out a breath. "And – I have not said this before, but Lorcan told me I should tell you – I am eager to try my hand at being a proper older sister. That is why I made the promise and would not release myself from it."

"Truly?" Elizabeth, who was standing next to Darcy outside the carriage, asked in surprise. "What exactly do you consider a proper older sister?"

Kitty took Fitzwilliam's hand and began her descent of the steps. "Well, Jane, of course."

Elizabeth laughed. "What exactly is it about Jane that qualifies her as the ultimate example?"

Kitty's eyes grew wide. "I have not offended you, have I?"

"No. I would agree that Jane is nearly perfect, and far closer to it than I shall ever be."

"I would disagree with that," Fitzwilliam inserted. "Mrs. Bingley is a lovely lady, but she is only one example of what a lady could or should be."

"Go on, Mr. Darcy," Elizabeth said. "I am fascinated to hear your explanation."

So was Georgiana. It was rare that she ever heard her brother talk about what a lady should be. He had always left those sorts of discussions for her to have with her aunt.

"Jane is so nearly perfect as she is because she is Jane. However, if Kitty were to fashion herself after Jane," he shook his head, "it would not work. I am not saying," he added quickly, "that Jane is not an excellent example to follow, but no one can be Jane except for Jane." His brow furrowed. "Do you understand what I mean? It is the same as if I were to try to be Bingley. That also would not work, and I would miss becoming who I am supposed to be, which, of course, is me with all my foibles and flaws."

He stopped just before they reached the steps where Richard and Lydia were waiting for them.

"I am just saying that what will make Kitty a proper older sister is being Kitty. Follow an example, but do not try to mold yourself into someone you are not." He smiled at Kitty. "You are a wonderful young lady, and I am delighted to have you for a sister and as a particular friend for Georgiana. Do not change who you are. Just be the best you that you can be."

Georgiana looked at Kitty whose cheeks were rosy and whose eyes glistened with tears. It was a perfect reflection of how she felt at her brother's words. She had always known Fitzwilliam to be a brother who cared deeply and wished for the best for her, and she knew that he had claimed Elizabeth's sisters as his own. However, she had never heard him put his heart about such things into words so well.

"Thank you," Kitty whispered.

His eyes turned toward Georgiana. "That is what I wish for all of my sisters." His lips tipped up into a small smile. "And I think they will all succeed. In fact, I am certain they shall." Then, he turned and continued up the steps to the house to greet Richard and Lydia.

"That appeared to be a very serious discussion," Richard said as he welcomed Darcy to his home.

"It was," was all her brother replied.

"Mother and Father, as well as Wes and Mary are inside. Lydia and I will wait for the Langleys." He winked at Kitty. "I thought you might be with them."

"I thought it better if she and Georgiana rode with us," Darcy replied.

"Do you not trust them?" Richard asked in surprise.

Darcy shook his head. "It is not that at all."

Georgiana knew that her brother's reason for

keeping her and Kitty from riding with the Langleys was her. He had not said so, but she knew, from how he avoided saying much of anything about Alfred, that she was the reason. She was glad, she supposed, for it meant she had not had to ride with the gentleman she loved and who found her wanting. However, she did feel sorry for Kitty. Of course, had Georgiana even hinted at such a thing to her friend, Kitty would have scolded her for feeling guilty. Kitty was too generous by half!

"It is my fault," she whispered to Richard when she gave him a hug.

"How so?" he asked as he darted a quick look at Darcy.

"I can tell you later," Georgiana replied.

"Has Young Alfred done something to harm you?" There was an edge of something dangerous to his tone.

"No, no, he has been a perfect gentleman," she assured him. "It is me."

"You will tell me later?"

She nodded. "So long as you promise not to be too angry with me."

"What have you done?" He tucked her hand in his elbow. "Lydia, my dear, I would like to walk with Georgiana until the Langleys arrive. Do you mind?"

She looked in his direction and smiled. "Not at all," she assured him and then, turned back to Kitty.

"Now," Richard said when they had reached the bottom of the steps and had turned to walk the opposite portion of the driveway to the way the carriages were arriving, "tell me what you have done."

With a sigh, Georgiana shared with him all that she had told her brother – from her realizing that she loved Alfred to the proposed and refused courtship and the discussion she had had with Alfred both about Wickham and how she did not meet his qualifications for a proper parson's wife.

Richard listened to it all in silence, save for a grunt or groan now and again, and when she had finished speaking, they walked on for a fair distance before he finally spoke.

"He is wrong. You are honest. That is why you could not elope with Wickham. You could not keep such a thing from your brother, and I know how much you have suffered over your deception. Not all your sorrow was due to Wickham's lies."

He shook his head. "However, I do not think that Young Alfred was saying that you have a glaring character flaw."

"But he did! I heard him say it."

Richard shook his head again. "We, gentlemen, do not always speak the same language as you ladies do."

"That is ridiculous! We both speak English."

"I will grant you that, but what you say and what we hear is not always the same, and so it goes with what we say and you hear."

"That makes no sense."

"I know. However, it is true." He chuckled. "Do not glower at me. Let me explain."

"Very well. Explain."

"Young Alfred will never find a wife who has not, at one point or another in her life, been deceptive. He knows this. However, he could not begin a courtship – not even a sham of a courtship – on dishonest grounds. His dedication to his profession and his aversion to disappointing his patron, who, by the by, happens to be your uncle, would not allow it any more than his nature would. He is an honorable young fellow. His heart is good. You would do well to have him as a husband – no matter what your brother might think."

Georgiana had been feeling quite reassured until that last bit. Once again, her heart was aflutter. "What does Fitzwilliam think?"

"He thinks that no one is good enough for you."

"That is also ridiculous."

Richard shrugged. "That may be, but it is true. However, if anyone were to win over your brother, I should think it would be Young Alfred or someone very much like him." He smiled at her. "Your heart has chosen well, Georgie, and any gentleman of Young Alfred's quality will forgive you for being led astray by a practiced charlatan such as Wickham. Trust your heart to tell you when you should share such a story with any gentleman who dislodges Young Alfred from your heart – that is if he does not come to his senses and secure you first."

"Do you think he might?" That was a hopeful thought!

Again, her cousin shrugged but smiled as if he knew more than he was saying. "He may. I have never found him to be stupid before. However, if he does prove himself to be lacking in good sense, then, I will have to agree with your brother and say he was not good enough for you." He pulled her into his embrace just as tears began to gather in her eyes.

How fortunate she was to have two such caring guardians. Her father had seen to her care very well.

"Now, shall we go greet your unenlightened fellow?"

Panic gripped her heart at the thought. To be honest, she had been relieved that her brother had insisted on her and Kitty riding with him. She had foolishly not paused to consider how she was to greet him once they were all here at Beaumont Park.

"Are you well?" Richard asked in concern when she did not move from her spot to walk on with him.

"I do not know how to behave around him, and I have been avoiding him for two days because of it." It felt good to admit that to someone. She had considered telling Kitty, but Kitty was betrothed to Alfred's cousin, and should Kitty slip and say something to Lorcan... Well, that was not a position in which Georgiana wished to place her friend.

"Be yourself. Whether he holds your heart or not, he is still your friend, is he not?"

"Yes, but..."

"You can do this."

She wasn't so certain she could, but then, what choice did she really have?

Chapter 11

From the window of his room at Netherfield, Alfred watched Georgiana cross the garden and walk down the path into the field beyond. Kitty walked on one side of her, and Lydia walked on the other. Whatever had caused her to be reserved and shy at Winsdale had disappeared somewhere between his home and Beaumont Park.

He turned away from the window and returned to getting ready to go riding.

Perhaps it had been seeing her aunt and uncle at Beaumont Park which had worked the magic. He knew she had not expected to see them until the wedding. However, Lord and Lady Matlock had decided that they would spend a week overseeing the improvements at Richard and Lydia's new home before travelling to Netherfield for the wedding, which meant they would be arriving in three days.

Or perhaps it was being in a setting with which Georgiana was familiar that helped her relax into her former self. While it unsettled him a bit that she would find his home, of all places, to be the place that caused her the greatest amount of anxiety, he was just happy to see her return to herself.

Indeed, watching her just now and hearing the laughter that had carried on the wind from the edge of the garden to his window made him feel lighter than he had felt in days. She was at ease, and, therefore, so was he.

Alfred buttoned his jacket and gave each sleeve a tug. Surprisingly, he had not found his time at Netherfield to be nearly so awkward as he had imagined it would be. There was far too much activity, and there were too many people around Netherfield for him to have an overabundance of opportunities to make a fool of himself by staring after Georgiana or woolgathering about her like he was doing now.

However, he was alone here. There was no one present to know that he had been watching her or thinking about her. That was why he found himself sitting in his room more frequently than was his normal wont. Usually, he liked to be part of whatever was going on or, at least, be where he could observe whatever was happening.

He grabbed his hat and exited his room.

"Are you going riding?" Lord Westonbury, Lord Matlock's eldest son, asked.

Alfred's brow furrowed as he took in Lord Westonbury's attire. The man was dressed for riding. "Why are you leaning against the wall outside my room?"

"I asked you a question first," Wes replied.

"Yes, I am going riding," Alfred answered. "Now, it is your turn."

"I was waiting for you."

"Why?"

"Mary is discussing babies with Elizabeth and Jane, and I am bored."

"Babies? As in more than one?"

Wes shook his head. "No, just Jane and Bingley's, so far as I know, but I was told that one can never be too prepared." He chuckled. "Although, if I were a betting man –"

"Which you are."

"Which I *was*," Wes corrected. "I think there

may be more than one baby which the ladies are discussing, though they are not willing to share that information with anyone else at present."

"Is that so? Would this potential infant be yours?"

Wes shrugged. "If I were to put a wager on a positive answer to that question, it would not be a small one."

Alfred chuckled and began to walk down the hall with Wes at his side.

"But not even I am supposed to know," Wes continued, "so do not say anything."

"Your secret is safe with me. I am not the sort who likes to gossip."

Wes clapped him on the shoulder. "You are a good man, Young Alfred. Now, where are we riding?"

Alfred had hoped to ride by himself. "Where is Lori?"

"Playing billiards with Bingley."

"And Mr. Darcy?"

"Reading."

"And your brother?"

"He is on his way to Longbourn, which is where Kitty, Georgie, and Lydia are going."

They stood at the top of the stairs.

"There is no one else," Wes said. "I am afraid you are stuck with me."

"Could you not entertain yourself?"

"I could," Wes replied as they descended the stairs, "but what fun is there in that?" He stopped and turned to face Alfred who was a step behind him on the stairs. "You have been spending far too much time alone."

"I enjoy spending time alone on occasion, and I have brought some books with me to study." Not that he had put very much effort into studying them. He had opened all of them at least once and even read a paragraph or two from one of them.

"I thought we might ride toward Oakham Mount," Wes said as he continued down the stairs.

"Where is that?"

"Do not fret. I have walked in that direction before."

"Is it far from here?"

"Not overly," Wes replied. "Ah, good, I see our horses are ready."

There standing in front of Netherfield were two horses, saddled and waiting for riders.

"I did not ask for a horse to be brought up," Alfred said. "I was going to walk to the stables."

"I do apologize," Wes said. "I took the liberty of seeing that we had mounts before I went to change. We can walk back to the house from the stables when we are done."

It would have to do. Alfred was going to have a companion for his ride, and his companion was going to lead the excursion. It was likely natural for Lord Westonbury to do so. He was, after all, a viscount and used to giving orders and arranging things. Therefore, Alfred agreed that a walk on their return might be best and swung up onto his horse.

~*~*~

"This," Wes drew his horse to a stop along a path which was not overly far from Longbourn and down which he claimed they would find Oakham Mount, "is where Mary and I had our first argument." He smiled as if it was a wonderful memory.

"Do you know," he continued, "in all my life, I had never had any other lady speak to me as Mary did that day." He tipped his head as if considering something. "Perhaps my mother had spoken to me in such a fashion, but never any pretty, young, unattached female." He chuckled and then sobered. "From our first meeting, Mary has always demanded the best from me. She never saw me as a viscount or a prize to be won. She saw me as a man who was wanting and who could be more than he was."

"That is an excellent thing to find in a wife."

"Indeed, it is."

They once again lapsed into silence as they rode side by side.

"Lori tells me that you still need a wife."

"I do not need a wife," Alfred retorted. "If you came riding with me to convince me otherwise, you have wasted your time." Lorcan had attempted to convince Alfred of that very thing in the carriage both on their way to Beaumont Park and to Netherfield.

While Alfred wished for a wife – a particular wife – he was still not ready to rush into marriage. A long courtship would likely be best, both for him to establish himself in his living and for Georgiana to experience a season or two. It might also make her brother more welcoming of an offer of courtship and help him see that Alfred was not playing with Georgiana's heart or attempting to marry her for her money if he was willing to wait so long to marry.

"Eventually, you will." Wes, true to form, seemed unruffled by Alfred's protest as he glanced across at him. "Lori said you wish to be established in your profession first."

"I do." Relief that his cousin had been listening to him washed over Alfred.

"How established?"

Alfred blinked. "My apologies, but what do you mean?"

Wes pointed to their right with his head. "We need to go that way. The view is best from here, or so Elizabeth says, and Darcy assures me that Elizabeth would know best about that as this was one of her favourite places when she was living at Longbourn." He stopped and dismounted, apparently, choosing to walk his horse the rest of the way.

When Alfred had joined him in walking his horse, Wes once again asked his question. "How established in your profession do you wish to be before you begin looking for a wife?"

Alfred studied Wes for a moment. It seemed like a natural question to ask, but the fact that the subject had been brought up at all had Alfred feeling uneasy.

"I had thought I would hold my position for a year or two and then begin my search."

"Why a year or two and not longer?" Wes had come to a stop and was smiling as he looked out over the land before them. "Elizabeth was not wrong. This aspect is excellent."

No, she was not. Alfred had to agree that the view from this spot was rather spectacular. He could see why someone would favour this place as a sort of retreat from the busyness of life.

Wes looked at Alfred expectantly.

"I think I would like to understand my situation completely and establish myself in an area before bringing a wife into my life. How can I help her find her feet in a new role if I am just as unsure of myself?"

Wes chuckled. "I find it difficult to believe that you are ever unsure of yourself. You have such a natural easiness about you."

Alfred kept his gaze on the vista before him. What Wes said was true to a point. Alfred had never truly felt ill-at-ease in any new situation, and if he had felt so, it was only for a short period of time. "I have never had to care for a wife before." He wished to do it well, and the prospect of doing so was somewhat imposing.

"Neither have I, but it really is not so daunting as it seems," Wes was watching him intently. "If you can care for yourself and your family – your brothers, mother, father, Ellen, Lily, Nathaniel, Lori..." He shrugged. "It is not so very different from that, and I would say you are far better prepared for taking a wife than most men are when they marry because you have planned not for yourself, but for her – whoever she may be." He chuckled. "Most men of my acquaintance think only of themselves when considering marriage. That is they do so until they meet the lady whom they wish to make their wife. Then, the good ones, shift their thinking." He shook his head. "We all know some who never consider anything or anyone but themselves, but that is not you."

"I appreciate your confidence in my abilities. However, I find I would be most at ease if I had a year or two of guiding my parish and learning the ins and outs of the living before I brought a wife into it."

Wes nodded. "That is understandable I suppose.

However, for the purpose of contemplation, let us say when you are in town during the season, you meet a lady who fills your every thought and dances away with your heart. Will you allow her to be lost to you because, according to the calendar you have drawn up, her arrival on the stage of life has occurred too soon?"

The lady of whom Wes spoke had already appeared well before Alfred was ready for her to do so. However, just because he had fallen in love did not mean he had to immediately marry, and he had adjusted his plan accordingly. Not that he was going to tell Wes any of that.

"If she is a gem of a lady with the sort of disposition for which I would imagine you would be looking, other men will notice." Wes's tone held a warning. "I wanted to harm your cousin when Mary seemed to prefer him to me."

Alfred chuckled. "Lori did mention something recently about calling you out because of your interference."

"Yes, well, I deserved it. I acted abominably." He turned and started leading his horse away from the view. He did not ask if Alfred was finished taking his fill of the vista, he just expected that Alfred would follow him.

At first, Alfred considered staying right where he was and allowing Wes to wander off without him, but then, he turned his horse and did as Wes expected as he reminded himself that today Lord Westonbury was choosing their path.

"What if you meet such a lady?" Wes had stopped right in front of him and was looking him in the eyes. "Would you ask her to wait two years?"

"It would depend on the lady." He planned to do just that very thing with Georgiana. Doubt poked at his heart, causing it to quicken its pace. Would she be willing to wait two years for him if he could persuade her to accept him at all?

Wes continued his careful observation of Alfred as the silence between them grew into something excruciatingly uncomfortable. It was almost as if the man was looking for something in particular.

"One year. I suppose any lady would be willing to wait one year if she loved you, do you not think?" Wes asked but then did not wait for a reply before continuing. "I mean, if she were to fall for another during that time, then, you could assume that she never truly loved you, and you would be spared from being locked in a marriage of unequal affections." He seemed satisfied with his reasoning and turned away from Alfred with a chuckle.

"You were thinking of someone," he said.

How did Westonbury know that?

Wes cast a look in his direction. "And you love her, for no one looks so horrified at the thought of another man stealing a lady from him as you did unless he loves the lady about whom he is thinking."

Had his panic at such a thought shown on his face?

Wes put a foot into the stirrup of his saddle and pulled himself up onto his horse. "I would think twice about holding to my plan if I were you. You really do not want to live a life of heartache and regret just because the right timing was not *your* timing."

He had a point even if Alfred did not wish to admit it.

"Remember, Young Alfred," Wes said while Alfred was settling onto his horse, "a wife can help ease a transition into a new life." His eyes sparkled with amusement. "If you do not believe me, just ask my brother. The ways in which his life has changed are not insignificant, but he has weathered it well due in no small part to Lydia." And with that, he clucked to his horse and was off.

Alfred sat looking after him for some time before nudging his horse to follow. The truth which Lord Westonbury had presented in a nonchalant fashion fell on him like an adversary attempting to wound him and make him compliant enough to be taken captive.

How self-important had he thought himself to be to think that he needed to be the one to find his way on his own so that, in his all-knowing greatness, he could help his wife? He had never viewed it from that vantage point before. It was startling and more than a little unsettling and humbling.

Images of Georgiana patiently following Lily through the garden at Winsdale mingled with memories of her humming as she studied a flower and captured it on paper. He thought of her gentle manners and sweet smile. He shooed a fly away from his face and considered her caring heart that seemed to feel the pain of others as if it were her own. And he knew. He absolutely knew that having her at his side would most certainly bring peace to him that no amount of foreknowledge about a living situation ever could.

He did not allow his horse to catch up to Westonbury's until they had nearly reached the stables at Netherfield. Instead, he held back and indulged his thoughts for so long as he could.

"What is your conclusion?" Wes asked as they dismounted in the paddock beside the stable.

"My conclusion about what?" It was a pointless question meant to put off an admission Alfred did not feel ready to voice.

Wes laughed. "You mean to tell me that you were letting me ride ahead of you not so you could think but so you could admire my form?"

Alfred chuckled. "Very well, I was thinking, and you might be right. I may need to reassess my plan."

That comment earned him a wide grin. "You could be persuaded to marry earlier then?"

Whether Alfred answered that question or not, Wes was going to assume he was right. He often did, unless someone proved him wrong. It was just how he was – confident to a fault.

"It would have to be the right lady," Alfred replied.

"Would the right lady be the one about whom you were thinking?" Wes pressed.

"Yes," Alfred admitted. Yes, it would have to be Georgiana, for he wished for none other — and not just because he wished to protect her but simply because he needed her.

Chapter 12

For the most part, it had been a lovely morning. Georgiana had spent a portion of it playing piano with Kitty, and then another portion of it trimming a bonnet in the corner of the sitting room while Kitty spent time with her Mr. Langley.

The other Mr. Langley – Mr. Alfred Langley – had spoken to Georgiana briefly, but then, he had disappeared to read in his room. He had been doing a lot of that lately. It was as if he were attempting to avoid being in company with anyone, though most especially her.

"What are you thinking about?" Kitty leaned toward her and whispered the question as they walked down the path toward Longbourn.

"Just the morning," Georgiana replied.

"I think it was a spectacular morning," Lydia said.

"So do I," Kitty agreed wistfully.

Georgiana laughed. "Of course, you both do! You had gentlemen who love you with whom to spend it."

And truth be told, she was beginning to feel a bit jealous of her friends' happiness, not to mention that of her brother, Mr. Bingley, and Wes. She was surrounded by happily besotted individuals, and she was happy for them. However, sometimes her happiness gave way to longing. It was not a profound discomfort that constantly made her wish to weep or anything. It was just a pang now and then. Most often when Mr. Alfred Langley decided to take to his room, as he had this morning.

"By this time next year, I am certain you will have your own gentleman," Kitty assured her. "You cannot be so rich and beautiful for nothing."

Again, Georgiana laughed. "I suppose I could always purchase a husband with the stipulation that he must dote on me always as both Mr. Langley and Richard do for you and Lydia."

"Oh!" Lydia cried. "You shall not have to buy a husband, and," she continued with some force, "we shall not let you fall prey to some fortune hunter. You shall be just as happy as Kitty and I are."

"Precisely," Kitty agreed. "And I would add that Mr. Alfred Langley already dotes on you."

"Yes," Georgiana agreed dryly, "that is why he flees the room so often."

"Ah! Is that it?" Lydia's tone was far too delighted for Georgiana to not feel some unease.

"Do you love," she lowered her voice to a whisper, "Mr. Alfred Langley?" Her voice returned to its natural volume as she continued. "I have noticed there was something about you that was not as it had been in town. However, I could not put my finger on it, but this must be it!"

Georgiana's unease had been warranted. Her feelings about Mr. Alfred Langley were not things about which she wished to speak. Kitty's arm held Georgiana's more firmly as if she understood that speaking about such things was not easy.

"It is not as if I will share such a secret with anyone," Lydia added when Georgiana did not speak.

"Not even the colonel?" Kitty asked.

"Will you share it with Mr. Langley?" Lydia retorted

"No."

Lydia gave her sister a look that said she very much doubted that.

"Mr. Langley is Mr. Alfred Langley's cousin, which would make it dashed awkward for him to know about Georgiana loving his cousin," Kitty argued.

"I did not say I loved Mr. Alfred Langley," Georgiana interrupted.

"Nor did you deny it," Lydia added.

"It matters very little if I do or do not love him," Georgiana said. "We would not suit. I think we had much rather stay as friends than attempt to be more than that."

Lydia's eyes grew wide as a smile suffused her features. "You do love him. I knew it. But, I shall not say a word." She tucked her lips in and pressed them together as if to say that they were sealed on the subject.

"I think the two of you would suit quite well," Kitty said. "I cannot think of another lady I have ever met who is so gentle as you are."

"But you know my folly," Georgiana whispered.

"And you know mine," Lydia said.

"But you are not marrying a parson, and you

did not deceptively plan an elopement," Georgiana protested.

"I considered it," Lydia said in a very matter-of-fact fashion. "If I had not fallen in love with my colonel, I might have actually run away to Scotland with Mr. Wickham." She shuddered. "Can you imagine?" She shook her head. "That would have been a most spectacular folly!"

"Indeed, it would have been," Kitty agreed. "Especially since you were only doing it as a lark. At least Georgiana was not going to run away with him for such a silly reason. She thought he loved her."

"Mr. Wickham is very persuasive," Lydia said. "He suggests a plan and smiles just so, and a lady forgets herself and believes whatever he says."

"That is exactly how he spoke to me — with his charming smile," Georgiana admitted, "and he also wore a most charming expression while he listened as if he truly cared about what I thought." She shrugged. "It reminded me of how my father treated me – and Fitzwilliam to an extent." She sighed. "But then, Mr. Wickham had spent a great deal of time with my father, so I suppose he knew how to act because of it."

"He is horrid!" Lydia declared.

Georgiana could not agree more. Mr. Wickham was a practiced deceiver who plied his game most cunningly. He had been agreeable and compassionate to her and from what she knew about Lydia's interactions with the man, he had been light-hearted and exuberant with her.

With it agreed that Mr. Wickham was indeed a horrid, horrid creature, they walked on in silence until Kitty broke it.

"I do not see how being deceived by one such as Mr. Wickham makes you less qualified to be a parson's wife. Indeed, I think it adds to your suitability for such a role. You have known sorrow and shame and when you add that to your natural gentleness, I would be most pleased to have you as my parson's wife. Do you remember Mrs. Flynn, Lydia?"

"Who could forget her and her pinched-together scowling face and harsh words!"

"Mrs. Flynn," Kitty explained to Georgiana, "was the parson's wife who was at our church before our current parson came."

"She likely groused her husband into an early grave," Lydia muttered. "That is why we needed a new parson. Her husband died."

"I take it she was not a pleasant woman?"

"Far from it," Kitty answered. "It was as if she expected everyone to be perfect, and if you were not – and Lydia and I were often not – she made certain you knew just how dire your sin was."

"She let *everyone* know how dire your sin was," Lydia amended. "She was the worst sort of gossip."

Georgiana's eyebrows lifted high. "Indeed?" She had heard stories, in general terms, of parsons who were not fit for the role which they filled, but she had never experienced such a thing. And she had never heard a parson's wife spoken about in such an ill fashion.

"I am not entirely opposed to gossip," Lydia said softly. "I find it challenging not to tell stories, but I vowed I would never tell the sorts of stories she told. And I have not."

"It is difficult not to share a tale, is it not?" Georgiana agreed.

She was not immune to telling a story now and again, though she had to admit that since Ramsgate, she had not told one scintillating tale to anyone. It was because the damage that a whispered tale might bring had become vividly real to her thanks to Mr. Wickham. She supposed that she would have to count that as a good thing which had come from her experience. However...

"It does not matter. Even if Mr. Alfred Langley and I did suit, he does not think of me in such a fashion."

"Then, make him love you," Kitty encouraged.

"How? I have attempted to be myself with him ever since Richard told me to do so at Beaumont Park, and it has not drawn Mr. Alfred Langley to me. If anything, it has caused him to run in the opposite direction."

"Richard knows you love him?" Lydia asked in surprise.

Georgiana smiled sheepishly while nodding. "He is my guardian."

"And you were not going to tell us?" Lydia gave her a pointed look.

"I was not going to speak about it to anyone else – ever. For, it is obvious that it cannot be."

Kitty squeezed Georgiana's arm. "I would not be too certain about that. I, for one, think you still have hope."

"Only because you want me to be your cousin," Georgiana protested.

Kitty shook her head. "No, not just because of that."

"What do you know?" Lydia demanded.

"Nothing for certain and nothing I can share."

There truly was hope?

"And I could be wrong," Kitty added quickly. "Though I pray I am not."

That made two of them. For a fleeting moment, Georgiana allowed her heart to hope that making Mr. Alfred Langley love her was a possibility, and then, she remembered their conversation in the garden at Brookefield.

"I still do not see it as a possibility. I think it is best if we just all realize that Mr. Alfred Langley and I will never be more than good friends."

They stepped to the side of the road to allow a donkey cart to enter Longbourn's driveway ahead of them, but it did not. Instead, it came to a stop.

"Miss Lydia, Miss Kitty," the handsome gentleman who drove the cart said.

"Mr. Webb!" Lydia cried with delight. "We have not seen you in an age!"

"Indeed, it has been since the end of last summer, which is very nearly a year ago."

"And are you once again visiting your aunt?"

"I am. In fact, I am on my way to procure an order for her from Meryton, but she insisted that I stop and give her thanks to your mother for the cake she sent for my arrival."

"You have not been here long, then, have you?"

"No, not at all. I just arrived the day before last."

"And Mama did not tell us? How odd!"

Mr. Webb chuckled. "You are no longer in need of a husband," he said with a wink.

Lydia beamed. "I most certainly am not. Will you come in and meet my colonel? He will be here soon."

Mr. Webb's brow furrowed for a moment. "Is he travelling without you?"

"Oh, yes," Lydia replied with a nod. "I told him I preferred to walk, and since walking such a distance would not be good for him, he is coming in a carriage."

Mr. Webb placed a foot on the reins and let them go loose in his hand. "May I ask why walking is not good for him?"

"Have you not heard? He was injured on his last assignment," Lydia said. "He is much better than he was, but walking three miles, twice in one day, did not seem like a good idea."

"I had not heard that your betrothed was injured. My aunt did not mention it when she told me your good news." He looked at Kitty. "Your beau was not injured as well, was he, Miss Kitty?"

Kitty giggled. "No, he is spending the day at Netherfield."

"Ah, I see. I do hope I get to meet him at some point. Lucky fellows, the both of them!"

To Georgiana, Mr. Webb seemed a very affable sort of fellow.

"May I be so improper as to ask for an introduction to your friend?" he said with a glance at Georgiana.

"Oh! I forgot in the excitement of seeing you," Kitty said. "This is our dear friend and new sister, Miss Darcy. Miss Darcy, this is Mr. Webb. His aunt lives just beyond Netherfield."

Mr. Webb smiled. "I had heard there was a Miss Darcy. My aunt did mention that. It is a pleasure to meet you, Miss Darcy."

"Likewise," Georgiana replied.

"Come in," Lydia said. "Just for a few minutes."

"I need to get to Meryton," Mr. Webb answered.

"But you did say your aunt wished for you to give her thanks to our mother," Lydia argued.

"And you will not give it to her for me?" Mr. Webb said with a laugh as he tightened his grip on his reins.

"You simply must meet my colonel," Lydia answered.

"Very well. I shall stay just long enough to meet your colonel." Giving a click and twitch of his reins, he got his cart moving and turned into the driveway toward Longbourn.

"He is handsome," Georgiana said when Mr. Webb was well away from them. "Does he have an estate?"

"He is, and he will. But he is not Mr. Alfred Langley," Kitty's tone was cautioning.

No, he was not Mr. Alfred Langley, but he was a possibility – a handsome possibility, which must be, at least, considered.

Chapter 13

"Mr. Webb is visiting his aunt," Lydia said once she had taken a place on a sofa next to Richard in Netherfield's drawing room upon their return from Longbourn.

Mr. Webb? Who was he? Alfred looked up from his usual hiding place – a book of sermons. He had chosen to *read* this book in the drawing room instead of his bedroom this afternoon since the ladies had not yet returned from Longbourn when he had first sat down, and he simply could not keep himself from the delight of seeing Georgiana for at least a few minutes. Of course, thoughts of her and how he might let her know about his intentions without angering her brother were what had kept his mind too occupied to do much more than turn a few pages in his book.

"Is he?" Mrs. Darcy said with no little amount of interest.

Whoever this Mr. Webb was, he was a person of note from the way both Mrs. Darcy and Mrs. Bingley seemed interested in the bit of news Lydia had shared.

"Has he found a wife yet?" There was a smile playing at Mrs. Darcy's mouth.

Mr. Webb was a bachelor, was he? As much as Alfred attempted to school his features, his left eyebrow would not remain impassive and insisted on rising slightly.

Kitty giggled. "No, he has not found a wife. Mama asked."

"Right before she sighed over not having any daughters left to promote to him," Lydia added. "Not that he was unaware of that fact anyway. His aunt had already told him of our happy news."

"Mrs. Bennet did, however, mention that Georgiana would be looking for a husband soon," Richard said.

"She is not out yet," Mr. Darcy inserted with a pointed look for his cousin.

"There is no need to worry about that," Richard replied with a chuckle. "Mrs. Bennet made certain

Mr. Webb knew all the particulars. No one will be allowed to approach Georgie on Mrs. Bennet's watch unless they are completely proper about it."

"I am glad to hear it." Mr. Darcy's features relaxed. "And what did you think of this Mr. Webb, Georgie? Is he someone of whom I need to be aware?" His lips curled into a teasing smile.

"Fitzwilliam!" Georgiana's cheeks were a lovely shade of pink.

Alfred swallowed to try to get rid of the feeling that his heart was in his throat. Was she interested in Mr. Webb?

"Is he handsome?" Wes asked.

"Unless he has contracted some horrid disease since I last saw him, then he is very handsome," Mary said with an arched brow for her husband. "And," she said, looking in Mr. Darcy's direction, "he is as kind and good as he is handsome. He has always treated all of us with the utmost respect, which is why Mama was always so disappointed when none of us did more than dance with him. Not even Lydia flirted with Mr. Webb."

"Of course, I did not!" Lydia cried. "He is not the sort of gentleman with whom one flirts unless one wishes to marry him, and I did not wish to marry him."

"He was too proper for Lydia," Mary muttered, earning her a gasp and a glare from her youngest sister. "However, he would not be now," Mary added.

"But now he is too late," Richard inserted with a kiss for his betrothed's fingers.

"Then, this Mr. Webb is a viable candidate for a suitor for *someone*?" Wes asked as his eyes bore into Alfred.

Had Lord Westonbury discovered that Georgiana was the lady of whom Alfred had been thinking when they were riding earlier?

"Oh, most certainly," Mrs. Bingley assured him.

"But there must be something wrong with him if none of you pursued him." The comment was out of Alfred's mouth before he could stop it. Heat crept up his neck as all eyes turned toward him.

"He is not wanting in any way," Mrs. Darcy said. "He is handsome and has a modest estate that will one day be his. He possesses no improper arrogance, nor does he have any disquieting habits."

Lydia nodded in agreement. "And he always smells lovely."

"I am still uncertain as to why none of you would pursue such a paragon of perfection," Alfred said.

"One does not pursue such a fellow just as one does not flirt with such a fellow unless one wishes to marry him," Lydia explained.

Alfred's brow furrowed. Miss Lydia was perhaps the most difficult of the Bennets to understand. "Does that mean none of you pursued him because you did not wish to marry a handsome gentleman with a reasonable fortune and who is all that is proper?"

"No," Mrs. Bingley answered. "I would have married Mr. Webb if he had stirred my heart in such a fashion, for I did consider it. However, my one advance of greeting him upon his entry to an assembly was met with his customary friendliness and exclamation of pleasure at having secured the first dance with me, which I told him I had saved for him, but that was it. He made no effort to encourage my pursuit." She shrugged. "I supposed it was his way of saying he was not interested in me, and so, I let it be what it was."

"Oh, yes!" Mrs. Darcy cried. "A fellow must not hold his cards too close to his chest if he wishes to encourage a proper young lady to reveal her desires. I know my friend Charlotte has always said that a lady should not be too circumspect with her feelings when hoping to secure a particular husband, but it is not just us females who should be so open. Would you not agree?"

"I would," Wes answered readily. "Though I would caution that arguing and provoking the lady who interests you is not the best way to reveal your affections." He chuckled and several others chuckled along with him, including his wife. "How about you Young Alfred? What are your thoughts on the subject? Your answers are always interesting, and since you are the only chap here who has yet to find a wife, I think we should all like to know how you see such a thing from your point of view."

"Neither Lori nor Richard are married." Alfred held Lord Westonbury's gaze. He really had no desire to talk about such a thing with anyone, let alone a room full of people – especially when one of those people was the lady he loved and had avoided speaking to on the subject of his feelings for her.

"They will be soon." Wes did not look away.

Instead, his half-smirk seemed to taunt Alfred, insinuating that he was too fearful to reply.

"There may be mitigating circumstances which hinder a gentleman from acting on his feelings." There that should be enough of a reply.

"Such as?" Wes pressed.

Alfred's eyes narrowed with displeasure. "Let us consider this paragon of perfection named Mr. Webb, shall we?"

Wes motioned for Alfred to continue, so he did while keeping his eyes purposefully on Lord West-onbury. "Suppose for a moment that he is introduced to a young lady, such as he was introduced to Miss Darcy today. And suppose that this young lady was not yet out just as your cousin is not, but Mr. Webb fell madly in love with her. What should he do?"

"Does she love him?" Wes's half-smirk had grown to full-size.

Alfred shook his head. "He does not know. Remember, Mr. Webb has just met her. Propriety says that he should not make his intentions known until she has been presented to society. Therefore, if he does tell this young lady that he loves her, he is no longer so proper as he once was, and he may find himself rejected either by the young lady or her family."

Wes's eyes lit with understanding and his head bobbed up and down. "I suppose you might be right." His eyes shifted to Mr. Darcy. "What do you say, Darcy? Is Young Alfred right?"

"I think I would rather hear what my sister has to say on that before I answer," Mr. Darcy replied.

"Me?" Georgiana squeaked.

"Yes, you know Wes is going to ask you after he asks me, and if you say exactly what I have just said, he will think you are trying to please me."

"But you know we agree on this. Mr. Clements was far too forward and did precisely what Mr. Alfred Langley is suggesting. You know that neither I nor you will be accepting his call."

"What she says is true," Darcy agreed.

"That does throw a wrinkle in things, does it not?" Wes scowled softly and rubbed his chin with a finger as if deep in thought.

"But what if this young lady has already, either through flirting or seeking out this gentleman's attention as a friend, shown some interest in him, and she is out?" Mrs. Bingley asked. "That is what happened with me. What could the reason for such a thing be?" She looked at Alfred expectantly.

Alfred shook his head. "I am not certain. Perhaps he is not ready to take a wife and does not wish to raise expectations when he cannot in good conscience meet them."

Mrs. Bingley, hmmed for a moment before smiling and saying, "But would it not be appropriate for him to present himself to this lady with the caution that he was not in a position to do more than admire her? I am certain if Mr. Webb had shared such a thing to me, I might have been willing to allow him to call on me so that we could see if we would suit once his situation changed."

"I for one am glad Mr. Webb was not so forthcoming," Bingley interjected. "For had he been sensible and spoken to Jane, I would be a sorry, sorry fellow to be without my dear wife."

"I would agree with that," Richard said. "If Mr. Webb had pursued any of the Bennet ladies, we," he made a circling motion with his finger to encompass the lot of them in the room, "would all be in danger of not having found the happy futures we have."

This comment was met with a hardy *Hear! Hear!* and a couple of *precisely's*.

"But," Georgiana said, "if Jane had felt more than a passing interest in Mr. Webb, would she not have waited for him? Would not love have pushed her to do more than just make one advance? Did she not do more to secure you?" she asked Bingley.

"I suppose you are correct," Bingley answered.

"And Fitzwilliam, would you have stopped attempting to secure Elizabeth after just one try? Or you, Wes, would you have given up on Mary so easily?"

Both gentlemen admitted that they would not have.

Georgiana's eyes rested on her brother. "Then, I suppose one only pursues ardently and persistently until one's heart is no longer engaged."

"Or until the object of one's affection belongs to another," Wes said.

"Yes," Georgiana agreed, "or until then. Do you not think so, Fitzwilliam?"

Mr. Darcy nodded slowly. "But what does one do if one loses the object of his or her affection?"

Georgiana's shoulders lifted and lowered in a slow deliberate fashion. It was as if she and her brother were having a conversation that held a deeper meaning than it appeared to have.

"I suppose, if this unfortunate person is a lady," Georgiana finally said, "she would be fortunate to have family who would not turn her out or a fortune of her own to establish her own household."

"And if she is not so fortunate?" Mr. Darcy asked.

"Then I suppose she will have to either learn to love again or simply content herself with a good situation. I am certain a sort of love must develop in such circumstances, does it not?"

She spoke as if she knew the feeling of unrequited love intimately. Alfred knew that she had thought Mr. Wickham loved her, but she had insisted that after some consideration, she had come to realize that her love for him was not for *him* but for the image of the man he pretended to be. Therefore, falling out of love, as she had put it, had not hurt nearly so much as she had expected. In fact, it had caused her little pain compared to the foolishness she felt at having been so easily led along. So, if she was not speaking about Mr. Wickham, then, of whom was she speaking?

"I suppose it is the same for a gentleman," Wes said.

Georgiana turned to look at her cousin and agree with him, but her eyes lingered for a moment on Alfred. Sadness shone from their depths. Was she? No, it could not be. Could it? Was this her one advance? Did she mean that she loved him?

No, no, he told himself. He was merely seeing that for which he wished. He drew a silent but deep breath willing his heart to stop racing. However, his unease would not go away, for he knew that if he was wrong and she was speaking about him and he did nothing to let her know that he loved her... He blew out a slow breath. She just might attempt to find contentment with another such as the handsome, perfect, completely proper Mr. Webb, and he could lose her forever. Bile rose in his throat at the thought, and he pressed his fingers hard against the book he held, imagining it was Mr. Webb's handsome features.

He needed air and space to think, and likely a good stiff drink or two. However, Mr. and Mrs. Bennet were to arrive shortly for dinner so drinking would have to wait. Air and space would have to do for now. He rose from his seat.

"I think I will get ready for dinner," he muttered and attempted to make a hasty escape. However, in his state of distraction, he did not see Dash who was lying on the carpet midway between where Wes sat on Alfred's left and where Georgiana sat across from Alfred.

Finding himself sprawled across the floor had not been part of his escape plan.

"Mr. Langley, are you injured?" Georgiana knelt beside him with Dash, who was sniffing at Alfred's face, at her side.

"I believe it is only my pride which has been hurt," he replied, although his left wrist was rather sore. He winced as he applied pressure to it while rising.

"One cannot be too careful." Wes grabbed his arm and helped him gain his footing. "Georgie, open the door for us."

"I am well," Alfred protested as he was moved toward the drawing room door by Wes.

"No, you are not," Wes hissed.

"But I am."

"I can alter that fact," Wes warned as they exited the room. "Georgie, if you will accompany us."

He did not wait for her to say she would do what

he asked. Instead, he started up the stairs with his arm still around Alfred's waist.

"Tell her," Wes said when they had gained the landing.

Apparently, Lord Westonbury *had* discovered it was Georgiana of whom Alfred had been thinking earlier today. Alfred darted a look over his shoulder at Georgiana, who was following behind them with Dash at her heels.

"Tell her, or I will." Wes released his hold on Alfred.

"Here? Now?"

Wes nodded.

"Her brother."

"Does that really matter?" Wes asked in a whisper.

"To me it does," Alfred replied.

"Were you listening at all just now?"

For a moment, Alfred feared Lord Westonbury was going to hit him, but then, as they came nearly to the door of Alfred's room, Wes turned with a smile to Georgiana. "Young Alfred refuses to tell me if he is injured, but he winced when rising, so I know he is. Perhaps he will tell you. I will wait at the top of the stairs."

And he was gone. Once again, Lord Weston-bury had given an order and expected it to be done.

"May I?" Georgiana pointed to Alfred's left hand.

He held it out to her. Arguing that he was well with Wes, when he suspected he was not from the way his wrist was still throbbing, was one thing. Arguing with Georgiana about such a thing was another. He could not bear to be dishonest with her even if it meant she would discover his injury.

"Does this hurt?" She moved his hand up and down.

"Yes," he admitted.

"And now?" she asked while moving his hand from side to side.

Again, he admitted that it did.

"Does your other hand hurt as well?"

"The palm stings, but other than that, no, it does not hurt."

"This wrist will need a compress, and you will likely need to not move it too much while it heals."

"I know. I suspected as much. It is not a serious injury." He should pull his hand away from her, but he could not do it. He had not held her hand since before he had left Ravincot, and he missed it. How he had missed it!

"Oh!" She released his hand and touched his face near his left eye. "You have a red spot here," she explained, stepping closer to look.

"It is only a small burn from the rug." He leaned closer to her.

She smiled at him. "What will Lily say?"

His lips brushed her cheek. "She will ask me if I thanked the pretty lady for her help." He kissed her cheek once again before whispering a thank you.

He should not kiss her. He truly should not. Not even if her lips were so close. But oh, how he wanted to! However, instead of doing as he desired, he rested his forehead against hers. "Wait for me," he whispered. "Do not pursue Mr. Webb. Please, wait for me."

"Forever," she whispered in reply, rendering all his good intentions worthless as his lips, finally, claimed hers.

Chapter 14

Alfred's was not the first kiss Georgiana had ever received, but the one she had received in Ramsgate was nothing to this kiss. This one stirred more than a small feeling of being wanted by a charming fellow. This one invaded every crevice of her heart and surged from there to spread throughout her body, causing a tingling awareness of being treasured by a gentleman of worth. When it ended, she did not move from where she was. She wished to stay forever encircled in Alfred's arms. The impulse to seek a quiet moment in her room to admonish herself for her behaviour never appeared as it had in Ramsgate. Even when she heard footsteps in the distance, she did not jump away. She had found where she was supposed to be, and nothing was going to separate her from this wonderful place of refuge. The place where she knew her heart would be forever safe.

"Georgiana."

Alfred's body stiffened and his arms fell away from her.

"Yes, Fitzwilliam," Georgiana said without turning toward her brother. She slid a hand down Alfred's left arm and lifted his hand gently.

"Did you discover what was wrong with Young Alfred?" Wes asked.

She nodded and only then glanced at her cousin and brother. "He will need a compress for his wrist and a bit of salve for the red spot near his eye."

Her brother scowled at her, but she could tell it was not a truly angry scowl. His eyes were soft. "It seems Mr. Langley also needs to schedule an interview with me." His focus shifted from her to Alfred.

"Yes, sir," Alfred said.

"Would you prefer now, after dinner, or tomorrow?"

"Whichever you find to be best."

Her brother's lips twitched. Why was he tormenting Alfred so? It was a wonder any lady ever received an offer if this was the treatment gentlemen faced from the lady's guardian.

"I say now, but I can go ask Richard which he would prefer," Wes inserted.

"That might be best," Fitzwilliam replied. "I think he would like to be present."

Wes was gone nearly before her brother had finished agreeing to the plan.

"Maybe we could go find a place to be that is not the hallway," Georgiana suggested. Alfred did not look well. His chest was rising and falling noticeably and there was not even a shadow of a smile on his lips or in his eyes.

"Where do you suggest?" Fitzwilliam asked.

"There is a lovely sitting room attached to my room."

"No," both Fitzwilliam and Alfred said in unison.

"It would not be proper," Alfred added. "Could we use Bingley's study?"

"I am sure he would allow it," Fitzwilliam said with a nod and a wave of his hand toward the stairs.

Alfred, whose hand Georgiana still held, moved to walk toward the stairs, and she began to go with him until her brother stopped her by placing his hand on her free arm.

"You should get dressed for dinner, Georgie."

Her head shook of its own accord as the words settled into her mind. She would not be dismissed from this conversation.

Fitzwilliam took her by the arm and drew her away from Alfred. "I will join you in a moment."

Reluctantly, Georgiana let go of Alfred's hand.

"Trust me," Fitzwilliam whispered.

"But he is injured, and we have not spoken about anything other than the fact that I am willing to wait for him," Georgiana protested.

"Trust me," her brother repeated.

She pulled the right corner of her bottom lip between her teeth and looked past him to where Alfred was just reaching the stairs.

"You love him?"

Her eyes darted back to her brother. "With every part of me."

"You are not out yet."

"I know, and so does he. That is why he asked me to wait for him."

Fitzwilliam grimaced. "My understanding is that Mr. Langley wishes to wait a year before searching for a wife – that is what he has told both me and Wes. Therefore, he may have been asking you to wait longer than a couple of months."

She waited for her brother to continue, but he did not. He likely wanted her to tell him her thoughts on waiting more than a year to marry Alfred. Did he expect her to be in a hurry to marry? She wasn't. She had been at one time, but she was not that foolish girl any longer.

"How long would you have waited for Elizabeth?"

He smiled. "Forever."

She had known he would say that. "That was my answer when Mr. Langley asked me to wait for him."

Fitzwilliam wrapped her in his arms.

"Whether I am out or not, I am his, Fitzwilliam. I always will be."

He squeezed her more tightly. "I am satisfied. I would not have you be any less happy than I am." He released her and took hold of her hands. "I would use all that is in my power, as well as all that is in the power of all those I could enlist to help me, to see you as happy as I am. Father asked me to protect you."

Tears gathered in her eyes as they did every time they spoke about their father.

"And I will be requiring the same from young Mr. Langley. Not that I fear he would not protect you with his life." His lips tipped into a smile. "After all, the man did offer himself to bees to secure a flower for you. However, the charge must be given. It is my duty."

"Could you do it gently?" She knew how imposing her brother could appear when he was speaking about duty. "Please?"

"I will do my best. Now, go dress for dinner, and I will speak to you in an hour before we go down."

She did as he requested, but she did not do it without a good amount of unease.

"Georgiana?" Kitty peeked her head into Georgiana's dressing room before Georgiana had even rung for her maid. "Are you well?"

"I am. Why do you ask?"

"Wes came down alone, whispered to Richard, and they both left the drawing room. I thought it might have something to do with you." She bit her lip and diverted her eyes.

"It does."

Her friend's eyes lit with delight. "And Mr.

Alfred Langley? Does it have to do with him, too?" There was a distinct note of excitement in her tone.

She studied her friend for a moment before replying. "It does, but I have a feeling that you already knew that."

"Oh, I did not know, but Lorcan said it likely did." She pressed her lips together and her eyes grew wide as if she had misspoken.

That was interesting.

"Which dress shall I wear tonight?" Georgiana asked.

A look of disappointment passed across Kitty's face, but she crossed to the wardrobe where Georgiana was looking at dresses.

"Perhaps something blue or green," Georgiana said.

"Green, most certainly the green muslin, and with these slippers," Kitty replied as she pulled out a pair of cream coloured slippers with an embroidered vine of rosebuds decorating them.

Georgiana loved that pair of slippers. "I should have every pair of shoes decorated with flowers."

"Surely not your boots!" Kitty cried.

Georgiana laughed. "No, not my boots."

"Perhaps you could just wear stockings with flowers on them when you wear your boots," Kitty suggested.

It was just like her to try to find a way to make whatever Georgiana wanted a possibility.

"Which necklace will you wear?" Kitty asked.

"I thought to wear the pearl one."

"This one?" Kitty held up a string of pearls that had a pearl pendant suspended from it and intricate metalwork between each stone.

"Yes, that was the one. Do you think it will go well?"

"I do." She placed the necklace on the dressing table and ran a finger over the stones. "It is beautiful."

"Thank you. Fitzwilliam gave it to me."

"He has very good taste."

"I suspect my aunt helped him choose it." She knew that Lady Matlock had done much to assist her brother in his role as her guardian.

"It is more beautiful because of it," Kitty said with a smile.

"Do you have your things?" Georgiana asked.

The Bennets were to dine at Netherfield tonight, as was becoming a regular practice. Therefore, when they had returned with Richard after their call at Netherfield, both Kitty and Lydia had brought their clothes for dinner.

"They are on your bed."

"Shall we dress, then?" Georgiana's hand rested on the bell pull.

"I suppose we should."

"I must meet with my brother before I go down for dinner," she called to Kitty who had gone into Georgiana's bedchamber to collect her things.

Kitty stood at the side of the bed. "Why?"

"I am not going to shout it across the room," Georgiana turned from the door to her dressing room and walked away from where Kitty could see her.

"Why?" Kitty repeated when, with her clothes in hand, she rushed into the dressing room.

Georgiana drew a breath and released it. "Alfred kissed me."

Kitty's eyes grew wide, and she squealed.

"He was still holding me when my brother found us."

This was met with clapping and a little dance of joy from Kitty. "I wondered why Mr. Darcy left the room so quickly when Lord Westonbury appeared at the door. Lorcan thought it had to do with you and his cousin." She clapped her hands one more time. "He was right. I was so worried you were going to like Mr. Webb and give up on Mr. Alfred Langley, but Lorcan assured me that no one was going to allow that to happen." She sighed as a smile suffused her face. "He was right."

Mr. Lorcan Langley seemed to know a lot about what was or was not going to happen with his cousin. "What do you think he meant by no one was going to allow that to happen?" Georgiana attempted to ask it as casually as possible.

"I am sure I cannot say." Her friend once again pressed her lips together.

"What do you know?"

"I cannot say," Kitty replied.

"You cannot or you will not say?" Georgiana pressed.

"Both. I will not say because I cannot. It is supposed to be a secret." She wore a pained expression. "I am truly beginning to despise secrets."

Georgiana laughed. "As am I!"

"I will only say this, and it is likely more than I should. Ask your brother. He knows all about it."

Georgiana sat down heavily on the stool in front

of her dressing table. What had her brother said? She was to trust him because... She went back through the conversation they had had in the hall-way.

"He would do anything to see that I was as happy as he was. That is what he told me," she added when Kitty looked at her in confusion. "When I was talking to him in the hall after he had sent Alfred to Mr. Bingley's study, my brother said that he would do anything to ensure I was happy."

Even pressing her lips together could not hide Kitty's smile.

"Am I right? Did he have something to do with Alfred kissing me?" She shook her head. "No, that is silly. How could he know that Alfred would kiss me?"

Kitty looked as if she was about to burst. "Did Mr. Alfred Langley only kiss you or did he also ask you something?"

"He asked me to wait for him and to not pursue Mr. Webb, and then, he kissed me after I had told him I would wait for him forever."

Georgiana's maid had arrived and was busy unfastening Georgiana's clothes.

"Was there any part of what happened that your

brother might have been able to hope would happen?"

Georgiana shook her head. "Perhaps he might have hoped that Alfred would present himself to me, but I dare say I do not know how he would know that."

"I am sure I do not either."

Well, that was no help! Silence fell over the room as she and Kitty removed the dresses they were wearing and put new ones on.

"Lorcan said that his cousin and Lord Westonbury went riding while we were at Longbourn," Kitty said eventually. "It would have been an excellent day for it. I think they went to Oakham Mount. It is beautiful there."

"Did they?" Georgiana cast a questioning look at her maid.

"I heard they did, miss."

There must be a reason why Kitty would mention such a thing. Surely, there must be a reason unless, of course, she was just attempting to fill the silence with some sort of news.

"Did they do anything else?" she asked Kitty.

"I could not say," her friend replied, though she

most certainly appeared as if she could say but was choosing not to say.

Georgiana once again turned a questioning look on her maid.

"When they returned, Mr. Alfred Langley went back to his room. He requested fresh water for his basin. That is how I know that, and then I heard that Lord Westonbury and the other gentlemen enjoyed some port and sandwiches in the billiards room and were not to be disturbed – unless, of course, it was one of their wives looking for them. That part was Lord Westonbury's instruction."

"That does sound like Wes."

"Indeed, it does, miss."

"I wonder what they were discussing?" Georgiana muttered.

"A successful mission of some sort, miss. That is what Tommy heard Lord Westonbury call it."

How odd! She would have to be certain to ask Fitzwilliam how he spent his day. Hopefully, he would be forthcoming enough that she would be able to ask him about all the strangeness that seemed to be happening at Netherfield.

Chapter 15

Alfred stood inside the door to Bingley's study. He did not close the door, nor did he take a seat. He just stood, watching the door, waiting for his humiliation to begin.

Of all the stupid things to do, he had to kiss her. He should be thoroughly displeased with himself, but, oh, it was a struggle to be upset at himself over such a delicious indulgence as a kiss from Georgiana. It was much easier to be agitated about being caught kissing her by her brother, and that was exactly how he felt. He rubbed the middle of his chest with his right hand. The tightness he felt there was excessively uncomfortable.

"Relax." Lord Westonbury entered the room and clapped Alfred on the shoulder while he gave his admonishment and added, "There is nothing to this," in a whisper.

Perhaps being called up for poor behaviour was no big thing for Lord Westonbury, but it was for Alfred.

"I do not think we need you," Richard said to his brother.

Wes took a seat and patted the chair next to him while holding Alfred's gaze and tipping his head toward it.

"I am not here for you," he said to his brother. "I am here for Young Alfred. Someone needs to see to him." Again, he nodded toward the chair beside him, indicating that Alfred should join him.

"I will wait," Alfred said.

Wes cocked a brow. "Richard, tell the lad to sit down."

Richard chuckled. "You may be seated, Mr. Langley. No one is here to call you out or see you flogged."

"Are you certain?" Alfred asked.

"Whether he is or not," Mr. Darcy said upon entering the room, "I am certain that no one means to do you harm. My sister would be greatly displeased if anything untoward were to happen to you."

The comment did extraordinarily little to calm

Alfred's unease, for it only meant that Mr. Darcy would be prevented from doing anything unpleasant by his sister's wish, not that the man did not wish to do something unpleasant.

"Now, will you sit down?" Wes asked.

"Why are you here?" Darcy asked Lord Westonbury.

"To see to Alfred," Richard answered.

"Does he need a guardian?"

"No," Wes admitted with a grin. "However, you must know that Young Alfred is unaccustomed to being in trouble."

"He is not in trouble," Darcy assured Wes. "Mr. Langley will be well even if you are not here."

"I am not leaving," Wes replied. "I wish to see what I started to its conclusion."

"What *you* started?" Richard laughed. "I think it is what Darcy started."

Alfred had perched himself on the seat next to Lord Westonbury and was watching each gentleman with interest. He had no idea what they were speaking about, but it seemed as if some sort of scheming was afoot and he was the unwitting victim.

Unfortunately, Mr. Darcy did not continue the

conversation that the Fitzwilliam brothers had begun. Instead, he settled himself against the desk, leaning there while he turned his gaze on Alfred.

"I believe you once told me that you were only Georgiana's friend."

"I did."

"And you said that you despise deception." His familiar scowl settled on his features.

"I do."

"Kissing my sister is not what I would expect from a mere friend."

"Nor would I if I had a sister," Alfred agreed.

"You also told me that you did not wish to court Georgiana – even though, I am told, she asked you to do that very thing."

Alfred blinked and darted a look at the other two gentlemen in the room. Neither seemed surprised by this information. "You all know about that?"

"We do," Richard said.

Wes leaned toward him. "She told them, and Darcy told me."

"When did he tell you?"

Wes shrugged. "Right before I decided to go riding with you this morning."

Ah! Things were beginning to make a modicum of sense, though only a modicum. "I see."

To Alfred, it appeared as if Lord Westonbury's conversation on their ride had been planned, though he was not certain of the purpose.

"Do you care to explain the seeming discrepancy between what you have told me and what you have done?" Mr. Darcy asked.

Alfred chuckled. "Honestly, no, I would not care to explain myself. However, I will – at least, to whatever extent I am able."

Mr. Darcy smiled, which, to Alfred's way of thinking, was much more promising than a scowl. "Proceed."

"As I told you at Ravincot, Miss Darcy and I are friends. That has not changed in its essential truth. I still wish to help put her at ease in new situations whether that is when arriving at a place which is unfamiliar to her or in a ballroom where the character of the attendees may be well-hidden." He shook his head. "She needs no real help in either situation other than to have someone standing with her, but what happened to her in Ramsgate shook her trust in herself."

"It most certainly did," Richard agreed. "It has

also placed a heavy weight of guilt upon her. She feels her responsibility far more greatly than she should."

Alfred nodded. He knew that. He also knew that it was a Darcy trait. "We have spoken about that."

"You have?" Darcy said in surprise.

"In a roundabout way, yes. It was after the incident with the bees."

Once again, Mr. Darcy smiled. "I knew I liked you."

"You do?" It was Alfred's turn to be surprised. He had been nearly certain Mr. Darcy did not like him and would rather see him gone.

Wes laughed as Mr. Darcy assured Alfred that it was true.

"I believe you have not finished your explanation," Mr. Darcy said once Wes had finished chuckling. "You have only repeated what I already knew – that you told me that you and Georgiana were friends."

"*Are* friends," Alfred corrected. "Our friendship has not been lost. It has only been altered." Pleasantly altered in Alfred's opinion. "I cannot fix on the moment when our friendship became something more. Indeed, I did not know it was changing until I was irrevocably in love, though I can remember the moment I realized the transformation had occurred."

"Can you?" Darcy asked with interest.

Alfred nodded. He was beginning to feel quite at ease. So long as he could keep Mr. Darcy smiling instead of scowling, he would be well. Or so he hoped.

"I nearly died from the shock of it." His lips curled up. "Do you remember the day when you arrived at Winsdale?"

Darcy nodded.

"One should not make a shocking realization while eating."

Darcy laughed. "Is that why you choked?"

"It is."

This information, of course, demanded a thorough explanation to satisfy both Lord Westonbury and his brother.

"I can understand how a fellow can find himself in love without knowing he is even in danger of such a thing," Mr. Darcy said, and the other two gentlemen murmured their agreement. "I am satisfied with your explanation."

"I have not finished."

Mr. Darcy's brows furrowed. "Then, please, continue."

"If you remember, there were two other things which I said to you in the billiard's room at Ravincot. One remains true, the other does not."

One of Mr. Darcy's eyebrows arched in question.

"At Ravincot, I told you that I did not wish to court your sister. That is no longer true. I do wish to court her. In fact, I would like to do more than court her. I would like to marry her. However, she must have a season, and I have a living to take up."

"Would a lengthy betrothal work?" Wes inserted. "I think we are past the point of courtship if he is kissing her, do you not think?"

Darcy's eyes shifted from his cousin back to Alfred. "Is that acceptable to you?"

"Only if it is agreeable to Miss Darcy."

"I dare say it will be, but we will wait to hear her answer. Please continue with what you were saying before my cousin interrupted." He gave Wes a pointed look.

Alfred looked around the group gathered with him. These were three of the men who would in a year's time be his brothers. While Mr. Darcy still scared him somewhat, he could not help but feel grateful to be joining their ranks. They were all men of noble character – even Lord Westonbury, though he was the most unconventional of the lot.

"Miss Darcy is, and always will be, safe with me. I would give my life to see that she was."

Mr. Darcy drew and released a deep breath as if a burden had been lifted. "My father charged me with her protection before he died. It is not a responsibility which I have ever taken lightly."

Oh, Alfred knew that without being told. Anyone who took a moment to watch Mr. Darcy when his sister was present should have been able to tell how protective he was of her. However, that was not the only way Alfred knew of Mr. Darcy's protection for Georgiana. He had also heard it in the way Georgiana had wished to keep her brother from worrying about her during her season.

"That is why I asked Wes to find out where your heart stood in relation to hers," Mr. Darcy continued. "I had hoped, from the time we talked at Ravincot, that you would be the one who chose her." He shook his head as if slightly bewildered. "She trusted you with her secret, and you proved your care for her by being there to put her at ease. I did not think that there would be a gentleman with whom she would ever feel so at ease and who was so giving of himself with no promise of anything in return. I had hoped there would be, but, knowing her fortune and connections, I was not certain one could be found."

He smiled. "When I could not chase you away with a scowl, my hope that you were the gentleman for Georgiana grew. Then, I discovered my sister loved you, and it became my ardent desire that you would love her in return, for I could only fulfill my promise to my father if Georgiana's heart found the same sort of happiness I have found with Elizabeth."

He pushed off from the desk where he had been leaning and everyone else also rose. "I have asked her to speak to me before we go to dinner. I will send her here to you so that you can present your offer." His lips tipped up one side. "Even if she is not out."

"I can wait," Alfred offered.

Mr. Darcy shook his head. "No, you cannot. Grasp your happiness and do not let it go. Not even for me." He stepped closer to Alfred. "Just do not grasp it improperly." His eyes bore into Alfred's. "Do we understand each other?"

"Yes, we do."

"Good. Then, I will go get Georgiana and tell her you have both my blessing and Richard's." He looked at his cousin who nodded.

Wes stepped so close to Alfred that he could feel Wes's chest against his back. "Kissing and holding hands are not improper," he whispered loudly.

"Wes!" Darcy barked.

"This is why I am here for him," Lord Weston-bury said with a chuckle. "He needs clarification."

"I am not sure he does," Darcy retorted as Wes followed him out of the room.

"I know Young Alfred better than you. He needs clarification," Wes continued down the hall.

Richard was the only one who remained in the room. He held out his hand to Alfred who took it.

"Treat her well."

"I will." He gave Richard's hand a firm shake in promise.

"I know, but I had to say it."

"Of course."

Richard moved toward the door but paused at the doorway. "By the way, Wes is right about kissing and holding hands, but never tell Darcy – or Wes – that I said so."

Once he was alone, Alfred closed his eyes and expelled a deep breath. That interview had gone better than expected. He now only had to wait to present his offer to Georgiana.

His offer to Georgiana!

His eyes popped open. He was going to propose to Georgiana. He was going to ask Georgiana to be his wife. A grin split his face. That for which he had long, but for which he had thought he would have to wait, was about to be his.

He paced the room, planning what he would say. He would speak first of their friendship. Then, he would speak of his love before finally laying out his plans for the future and asking her to join him in them.

However, when she appeared at the door on her brother's arm, all his plans were forgotten. But was that not how it had been since he met her? His plans had been doomed from their first stroll in Brookefield's garden – and happily so, for any plans without her in them would have been a scheme destined for misery. He knew that now.

"Fifteen minutes," Mr. Darcy said as he closed the door to the study.

"Was Fitzwilliam kind to you?" Georgiana asked before Alfred could utter a word. "He says he was."

"He was excessively gracious."

The comment earned him a smile.

"He even said he liked me."

She giggled. "He told me that as well."

"Then, it must be true."

"Indeed, it must." She pulled her bottom lip between her teeth and clasped her hands in front of her. "He said you wished to speak to me."

"I do." He took her hands. "It seems I was a bit too hasty when I refused to accept your offer to court you in earnest."

Her brow furrowed. That was not how she was to respond.

"I apologize. Perhaps that was not the best way to begin." He stepped close to her and placed his injured left hand on her cheek. "I love you."

There. That smile was what he had hoped to see.

"I shall always love you, Georgiana. May I call you Georgiana?"

She nodded. "Of course. You may call me whatever you wish."

"May I call you mine forever and always?"

Her lips parted on a gasp. "Are you asking me to marry you?"

"That is what I am attempting to do, though apparently very poorly. Let me try again. Will you marry me?"

"When?"

It was not a *yes*, but it was also not a *no*. And she was still smiling. "At the end of the season."

"I do not need a season."

"Yes, you do, my love, for you and everyone else needs to see what I see." He wrapped his uninjured arm around her and pulled her close.

"What do you see?" Her right hand came up to rest on his heart while her left arm encircled his waist.

He paused for a moment to study her eyes. How did he put into words all that he saw in her? "I see my beautiful, charming friend who is quite capable of carrying herself with grace and dignity through the ballrooms and drawing rooms of the season and discerning with her keen mind and gentle heart who is and who is not worthy of her companionship."

"You see me like that?" There was no little amount of surprise in her tone.

"I do." Though that was only partly what he saw when he looked at her, it was the part which he suspected was the most important for her to know as it pertained to her fear of the season.

"But what of my dishonesty?"

He blinked. "What dishonesty?"

"I planned secretly to elope, and then, I asked you to pretend to court me."

She was concerned about that? Did she think he expected perfection? "I have been pretending to read in my room when I was really thinking about the lady I was attempting to avoid for fear of her brother."

Her brow furrowed again. "You were hiding from me?"

He nodded. "I was being completely dishonest with myself about my feelings for you until your cousin pointed them out to me this morning when we were riding. I knew I loved you. I could not lie to myself about that. I just thought I could ignore that fact, as if it were not true, until such time as recognizing it and acting on it fit into my plans. It was a foolish lie to believe." He pressed a kiss against her surprised brow. "None of us are perfect."

"Then, you do not find me wanting?"

"Wanting? Goodness no!" How did she think that?

Her smile returned to her face. "Richard was right. I should have known he was. He usually is."

"I do not understand."

"I will tell you later," she promised, "for, at present, my brother is likely staring at his watch counting the minutes, and I would very much like for you to kiss me."

He shook his head. "You have not answered my question. Are you attempting to avoid my offer?"

"No! No! Not at all! I will happily allow you to call me yours both now and forever."

"Is that a yes?" He smiled teasingly at her.

"Yes, Alfred – may I call you Alfred?" Her lashes fluttered.

He chuckled. "You may call me whatever you wish."

Her expression grew more serious. "Then, allow me to call you my love and my betrothed."

"With pleasure," he said as his lips descended to hers, claiming them and her as part of his wonderful, happy future.

Chapter 16

Groups of chairs, brought out from the house, dotted Netherfield's garden here and there. Some groups were larger, and some, such as this one, the one in which Georgiana had chosen to sit, were more intimate and consisted of just two chairs. It was in the second, and currently unoccupied, chair next to Georgiana in this group where Kitty took a seat.

"What are you doing?" Kitty asked.

"Watching my cousin and his new wife," Georgiana replied with a smile. "He has improved greatly, has he not? His scar is not so noticeable as it once was, and, if Lydia had not insisted that he carry his walking stick, he would not be leaning on it now."

"I do not think I have seen him stumble once in

the whole time we have been together at Netherfield," Kitty agreed.

"Neither have I." Georgiana peeked around to make certain she was not going to be overheard. "He is nearly who he used to be, and I do not mean physically. He smiles and teases as he used to."

Richard had never lost his smile or his ability to tease, but for a time, his eyes had held a shadow of something which seemed to hold him back from fully immersing himself in frivolity. That shadow had lifted completely and now when he smiled, every inch of him seemed to feel the joy of the action.

"He is in love," Kitty said. "And love can work miracles."

Georgiana nodded. "It seems it has most certainly helped Richard heal. Your sister has been very good for him."

Lydia was most attentive to his needs and often anticipated them before they even arose. Such as now when a guest approached where Richard would not be able to see him. Lydia had effortlessly drawn the guest to where Richard could see him without that guest being any the wiser that he was being herded to the proper position.

"Did you see that?" Georgiana asked Kitty, who nodded.

"She has always been exceptionally good at orchestrating things to her liking. However, it was not always so welcomed when we were growing up," Kitty said with a laugh.

"Is it not amazing how things work? What you saw as a defect in a younger sister is precisely what was needed for Richard."

Georgiana's mind went back to a conversation she had had in a different garden. She remembered how Alfred had spoken about not knowing why some things happened and finding it hard to trust that there was a purpose. A moment like this while sitting in Netherfield's garden during Richard and Lydia's wedding breakfast was just the sort of thing which helped her believe that things did happen for a reason. She would have to mention it to Alfred later.

"You are thinking of your Mr. Langley. I can see it on your face," Kitty teased.

"How can I not think about him on a day such as today? This will be us in a year. Are you still certain you wish to wait until June to marry? Your promise is complete. You brought me just the right gentleman. I no longer have to worry about selecting the wrong husband."

Kitty laughed and shook her head. "I am determined to have a season with you before either Lorcan and I or you and Alfred marry." Her eyes grew wide, and she gasped before a smile suffused her features. "We should marry on the same day."

"A double wedding?"

Kitty's head bobbed up and down enthusiastically. "We could marry in London before we leave at the end of the season, or we could marry…" Her brow furrowed. "I am not sure where else would be best, to be honest."

"I think London would be perfect," Georgiana said. "We will all be there, although I am not certain about Ellen and her children."

Kitty shook her head. "We will ask our Mr. Langleys. They will know what is best. But we must marry together. I would dearly love to share such a day with you."

"And I would be happy to share it with you. I never thought I would have a sister with whom to share my wedding day." Indeed, Georgiana had never expected to have any sister other than the lady her brother married. "Are you not excessively pleased that my brother married Elizabeth?"

"I could not be more delighted," Kitty agreed. "Do you want to come with me to find Lorcan? Alfred is likely with him."

"Alfred is here," Alfred said from behind them. "And Lori is with me. They had just brought out a new pitcher of lemonade when I was at the house, so I have brought you a cup if you would like it, Georgiana."

"Thank you." Georgiana took the cup from him and took a sip.

"I did not bring any for you, Kitty, because I knew you had just had some not long ago," Lorcan said apologetically.

"I do not wish for any, so you have done just as you should have." She rose from her chair and motioned to Alfred to take it. "I would like to walk with Lorcan, for there is something which I would like to discuss with him." She winked at Georgiana who nodded.

"Have you two been making promises again?" Lorcan asked with a laugh.

"No, but we do have an idea." Kitty wrapped her

arm around Lorcan's. "I will tell you all about it as we walk."

"Is it a devious plan?" Alfred teased as his cousin and Kitty moved away from him and Georgiana.

"Not at all. Kitty suggested that it would be lovely to share a wedding with us. I know we have not decided on a date or any of the details for our wedding, but..." She watched his face. There were no signs as to whether he liked the idea or not. "What do you think?"

"It is something to consider," he replied before a smile made his dimples appear. "I am not opposed to it. I will marry you whenever and wherever you wish, my love." He held up a finger. "But not until after you have your season."

"Kitty is not marrying until June. She assures me that on that she will not be moved. Much like you, she insists on my having a season first." How fortunate she was to have people who loved and cared for her so much that they insisted that her needs came before their own.

Alfred chuckled. "She is a good friend."

Georgiana could not agree more. She had truly been blessed.

"If you are done with your lemonade, would you

care to take a walk with me? We have so few days left to do so before I must leave."

The thought of his soon departure for Brooke-field caused her heart to pinch. "I wish you did not have to leave."

He took her empty cup from her. "I know, but it is necessary. I have a profession that comes with duties that require my attention. I would not leave you for any other reason."

She knew that, and she would not take him from what needed to be done. However, knowing he was only seeing to his responsibilities did not make the ache in her heart go away.

"I must learn to bear it," she said.

There would be times when he would not be able to be with her during the season as well. While he had a curate, who would be under him, Alfred was not the sort to pass all his responsibilities on to another just so he could indulge himself in the sea-son. She admired that about him. It was very like how both her brother and Richard were.

"I would say that I also need to see to readying our home for you, but I think your aunt has decided that that is her role and not mine." He chuckled. "That is likely for the best since I am not well-versed on décor."

Lady Matlock had been overjoyed to hear that Georgiana and Alfred were to marry. She had even confessed to hoping for such an outcome after observing them at Brookefield in the summer.

Lord Matlock had been more reserved in his delight, but he had not been any less pleased than his wife. While he admitted that it would, at first, be awkward to have his niece as his parson's wife, he could not help but be too fond of her to overcome any discomfort such an arrangement posed for him. Truth be told, he had said, it was always going to be challenging for him to see Georgiana married and who she married had nothing to do with that. It all came down to his loving her as dearly as he would have had she been his daughter.

"You realize that, once we marry, my aunt will be your aunt as well."

"Yes, I am aware of that fact." He blew out a breath. "However, it is still a bit much to contemplate. I never expected to marry poorly, but I had not thought I would marry the niece of an earl." He placed Georgiana's empty cup on a tray that a footman carried.

"All will be well," she said as she wrapped her arm around his.

"So long as you are by my side, I know it will be." He covered her hand on his arm with his hand. "Have you spoken to Richard and Lydia yet?"

Georgiana nodded. "I did while you were inside and before I took a seat to wait for you." She smiled when Richard bent to kiss Lydia. "They are so happy."

"As they should be." Alfred lifted Georgiana's fingers to his lips. "And as we are and will be."

~*~*~

As planned, two days after Richard and Lydia's wedding, Alfred left Netherfield with Lord and Lady Matlock to return to Brookefield and take up his living. For a month and a fortnight, the mail service between Netherfield and Brookefield was rarely without a letter to carry in one direction or the other.

There was news of rooms that were being refreshed under Lady Matlock's watchful eye at the parsonage. There were details of days spent making dresses and trimming hats, along with reports on how Georgiana was progressing on various pieces of music. There was even one happy letter that arrived at Netherfield announcing the birth of a brother for Lily and Nathaniel.

Interspersed with these reports on the happenings of life, were discussions of the more philosophical and theological matters of life, and, of course, no missive was complete without, at least one mention of either Georgiana's love for Alfred or his for her. Truth be told, a letter bearing only one such comment would have been a very rare and worrying thing, so it is, therefore, a blessing that no such worry ever arose.

Then, came the happy day when Alfred was returned to Georgiana. The reunion was as would be expected between young lovers. Kisses were shared and secretly stolen. Strolls along the garden paths at Netherfield were only neglected on days when the weather did not cooperate. Darcy scowled and smiled in equal measure while he watched his sister and the gentleman who had claimed her heart and promised her a happy future.

The reunion would not be a long one. Alfred was only in Hertfordshire for a fortnight before he would need to return to Brookefield and before Georgiana would be going to town to be fitted for gowns and to take a few lessons from her dance

master to make certain she was thoroughly prepared to enter the season.

However, before that, Georgiana was to make
her first foray into society in the assembly rooms in
Meryton.

"I have something for you," Alfred said to Georgiana before she disappeared above stairs to pre-
pare for the assembly.

"You do?"

He nodded and took her hand as she started to
ascend the stairs. "It is in my room, so you will
need to wait in the hall for me to retrieve it. I have
been assured by Kitty that it will match your dress
perfectly."

"Kitty knows about this gift?"

"She does and so does your brother."

Alfred was exceptionally diligent about being
proper. That is, he was proper according to Lord
Westonbury's definition, which included kisses
and holding hands, and from the number of times
Georgiana had seen her brother look the other way
when Alfred kissed her, it seemed her cousin was
not her only relation who held to such a definition
of what was proper for a betrothed couple.

"Wait here," he said when they reached the top of the stairs.

He was gone and back so quickly that Georgiana suspected that the gift he held had been waiting next to the door.

"It is nothing overly extravagant, but I think it is fitting." He opened the box he held in his hand, revealing a small flower pendant made of five diamond petals and a diamond center on a gold chain.

"Oh, it is lovely!" She ran a finger over it.

"That is not all."

Her eyes lifted from their study of the beautifully delicate necklace he had presented to her to his face.

"Take the necklace."

She did.

"This is for your hair." He took a small bag from his jacket pocket. Then, he took the box from her hand and replaced it with the bag.

Georgiana peeked into the bag. "Is that...?" She could not believe what she was seeing. "A bee?"

"It is, indeed," Alfred said proudly. "The prettiest flower in the garden always attracts bees, does it not?"

She laughed. "It does. This is perfect." It was a beautifully sparkly bee affixed to the top of a pin.

"I chose it, of course," he said as she twirled it this way and that, watching the light catch the wings and body, "as a reminder that I will always protect you."

Could any lady ever find a more perfect gentle‑ man to love her? Georgiana thought not. She tucked the bee back in its protective pouch before leaning forward and pressing her lips to his. "Thank you," she whispered, "and not just for the necklace or hairpin. For loving me."

He pulled her to him and kissed her. Then, with a sigh, he released her. "Go. Get ready. You have an important night ahead of you."

Two hours later, Georgiana arrived at her first official soiree. From this point forward, she would be included in all the invitations her brother received for various events. No longer would she be waiting. No longer would she be considered as not quite fully grown. From this moment forward, she would be Miss Darcy of Derbyshire, debutante and full member of adult society. A little shiver of excited nervousness coursed through her as she handed her wrap to a maid who would see to it while she danced.

"Are you ready to introduce the world to the Miss Darcy I see and love?" Alfred held his hand out to her.

"I think I am." There was a little fizzing of nerves in her stomach, but it was not unbearable at all.

"All will be well," he assured her as she placed her hand in his.

And she knew it would be, for how could it be anything but wonderful when she had Alfred at her side? Her free hand touched the pendant of her necklace, and she knew that, beneath it, her heart was and always would be safe for it had chosen to love a good man.

Alfred cocked an eyebrow in question.

She smiled. "I am ready, my love. Lead on."

And with a squeeze of her hand and a whispered "I love you", he did just that, leading her to the door of the assembly room and stepping with her into a future filled not only with dances and dinner parties but also with an abundance of love and joy.

Epilogue

[June, Five Years Later, at Brookefield, Lord Matlock's estate]

Rain had dampened the garden at Brookefield for three days, but it had not touched the exuberance found inside the nurseries, except to make one little fellow particularly testy. Four-year-old Arthur Henry Fitzwilliam, future Viscount Westonbury, had chattered nearly constantly for a month before his cousins arrived about how he and John Bingley were going to play with Uncle Darcy's dog, Dash, in the garden. To have such a treat as running after a dog and throwing sticks for Dash to chase taken from him did not sit well with Arthur.

Though the house was filled to overflowing with cousins and aunts and uncles, both the sort that were related directly by blood and those who were more loosely related but still a part of the large family gathering at Brookefield, Arthur sat by himself on a window seat, staring out at the disappointingly wet weather.

"You look just as grumpy as those clouds out there." Alfred sat down on the window seat next to Arthur.

"I like sunshine," the boy said glumly.

"So do I," Alfred agreed. "And a good breeze to make the leaves dance on the trees. They are dancing now in the wind, but they do not look so happy as they do when the sun is shining, would you not agree?"

Arthur nodded.

"You know if your mother would allow it and we were taller than Goliath, we could go outside and peek into the nursery to see what the raindrops see."

Arthur turned his attention away from the window and toward Alfred. "The raindrops look into the windows?" The child's eyes were wide with wonder.

Alfred chuckled. "No, but if they could, do you know what they would see?"

Arthur shook his head and turned to face the room.

"They would see Aunt Georgie kissing baby Violet's head before tucking her in for a nap." He bent down so that he was seeing the room from Arthur's vantage point. "And there is Rosanna at her mama's ankles, feeling jealous of her younger sister. What do you see?"

"There is Mama and Papa with Philip." He pointed to his mother, father, and younger brother. Lord Westonbury spent a great deal of time in the nursery with his sons and whichever of the other children of the family happened to be visiting Brookefield at the time. Currently, he was admiring a block before handing it back to his son and sending him on his way back to play with his cousins.

"And look, Uncle Darcy is peeking his head in." Alfred nodded a greeting to his brother-in-law. Darcy and Alfred had become good friends over the past five years, and Alfred no longer had to endure one of Darcy's scowls.

Darcy crossed the room to where Alfred sat.

"Scoot over," Arthur said, giving Alfred a gentle nudge. "Please."

Alfred scooted and Arthur followed suit, plastering himself next to Alfred.

"Sit with us," Arthur said to Darcy.

One of Darcy's eyebrows arched.

"Please," Arthur added.

"Much better," Darcy said before taking a seat. "What are we doing?"

"We are seeing what the raindrops would see," Arthur replied.

Darcy shot Alfred a questioning look over the top of his nephew's head. "And what are the raindrops seeing?"

"Children having fun," Alfred answered. "It is a much cheerier site that they are seeing through the window than we are seeing when we look outside."

"Ah." Understanding suffused Darcy's features. "John just arrived."

"John is here?" Excitement laced Arthur's voice. John Bingley was a full nine months older than Arthur and was, at present, Arthur's best-loved friend and cousin.

"He brought Oliver."

"Oooh!" Arthur cried. "May we play with Oliver?" He looked between Alfred and Darcy.

"You will have to ask your parents, but Aunt

Jane said that it was a fine plan if you played in the green sitting room down the hall. She does not want the cat in the nursery."

Arthur popped off the window seat and raced across the room to his father, who scolded him for not being careful around the babies. "You nearly stepped on Fanny's fingers."

"But I did not step on them," Arthur protested.

"Apologize to your sister."

Arthur scowled but did as he was told.

Alfred chuckled.

"Hearing Wes scold his son about something he would likely have done himself never grows old, does it?" Darcy asked.

"No, it does not."

Lord Westonbury still enjoyed stirring up trouble, but he was firm with his son. Arthur would be a considerate gentleman – even to his sister. Mary's lessons about how to treat a lady had not fallen on dry soil. They had taken root and flourished. Lady Westonbury, at her husband's urging, had taken on the patronage of a half dozen charities which helped women and children in a variety of ways.

Rumor had it that Lord Westonbury was writing a conduct book for young men – his sons and nephews, in particular. However, try as they might, no one had been able to find written evidence of such a project. However, the occasional whispered, "that should be in your book" from Lady to Lord Westonbury was enough to fuel the flames of speculation.

"Are you staying in the nursery with Wes?" Darcy asked.

Alfred shook his head. "No, I was just waiting for Georgie when I saw Arthur frowning at the window."

"He does like to sulk when things do not go as he wishes them to go, does he not?"

"Indeed, he does," Alfred agreed as he rose from the window seat. "Will your wife expect a report about your son?"

"I told her I would look in on him, and from all appearances, he looks well."

Thomas Darcy was busily building some sort of block fortress with his cousins, Philip, Wes's second son, and Henrietta, Richard's daughter.

"How is Georgie feeling?" Darcy whispered.

"She is constantly hungry but not ill as she was with Rosanna and Violet. She is certain this one must be a boy from how hungry she is. And how is Elizabeth?"

"You would never know she was pregnant if it was not for the swelling of her abdomen."

"And is the baby well?"

Darcy nodded. "We are beyond the most fearful point, and Elizabeth says this baby is more active even than Thomas was."

"I am happy to hear it. We will, of course, still remember you in our prayers."

This was Elizabeth's third pregnancy. Her first had ended abruptly the month before Georgiana's first season. Despite the devastating loss, Elizabeth had insisted on being present in town for Georgiana and Kitty. Both she and Darcy had found comfort in caring for their sisters, and by the time both Kitty and Georgiana were standing with their Mr. Langleys before the parson four years ago, Darcy and Elizabeth had been blessed with a second pregnancy. This one would be successful and brought to them their beloved son, Thomas.

"This is quite the brood is it not?" Mr. Bennet stood at the door to the nursery surveying the activity and holding Celia Bingley. Her older sister Edith had already found her way to the dolls.

"And it will only become more of one when Lori gets here with his two boys," Alfred answered.

"Elizabeth has told me your secret," Mr. Bennet whispered to Alfred. "I am hoping for another girl."

Alfred laughed. "Georgiana thinks it is a boy."

Mr. Bennet passed his granddaughter to her nursemaid. "I love all my grandchildren, but to see my daughters in the faces of my granddaughters..." He shook his head. "That is truly delightful."

"I would love to have a daughter who looked like Elizabeth," Darcy agreed.

"Then, we will both hope for such a thing." Mr. Bennet sighed. "However, I have learned that what you hope for and what you get are not always the same, but, and Young Alfred will appreciate this, what the Good Lord gives you is exactly what you are supposed to have. Despite all my wishing, I never had a son, though I have six now."

Alfred had only once corrected Mr. Bennet by telling him that he only had five sons. Mr. Bennet had told him in very direct terms that Georgiana was a sister to his daughters and, therefore, that made Alfred a son and no one was going to dissuade him of the notion. Strangely, the man never claimed either of Bingley's sisters or their husbands as his children. It was only Georgiana and Alfred who had been gathered under Mr. Bennet's wing in such a fashion.

Alfred attributed that fact to the closeness of Kitty and Georgiana. Correspondence passed regularly between the parsonage at Brookefield and Ravincot, and visits were made so often as was possible. Alfred's mother and Lily were happy for the frequency of visits between the two ladies since it meant that Alfred and Georgiana always included a visit at Winsdale.

Georgiana wrapped her arm around Alfred's. "I am ready to go wait for Kitty."

Waiting for Kitty did not happen, for just as Georgiana and Alfred were descending the stairs at Brookefield, Kitty and Lorcan were entering the house.

"Allow us to apologize again for not having been here yesterday," Kitty said to Lady Matlock.

Yesterday, a messenger had delivered a note informing them that the Langleys from Ravincot would be a day late in arriving because one of their twin boys had fallen when climbing a set of shelves and had required a visit from the surgeon.

"How is Emory?" Lord Matlock asked.

"As you can see, he is bruised, and he needed three stitches, which he finds bothersome. However, he seems well other than that," Lorcan answered. "Curtis has been a comfort to his brother. Is that not right, son?"

Curtis was the less forward of the two Langley boys and was standing close to his father's side, while Emory was pulling on his nurse's hand, wishing to be off doing something. The fall had not slowed him overly much.

"Emory," Lorcan barked and his son stood still.

"Their cousins are in the nursery. If you wish, they can join them straight away instead of being bored by us adults," Lady Matlock offered. Then, she bent down and greeted both youngsters before their nursemaids took them upstairs.

"Not all of the cousins are in the nursery," Lord Westonbury whispered when the boys were well away from the adults. "John and Arthur are tormenting a cat."

"They are playing nicely with Oliver," Jane said as she joined them. "Have I missed the hugs?" she asked.

"Not at all. I have not yet hugged anyone," Wes said. "I think I shall start with my wife."

"Reginald," Lady Matlock scolded with a laugh, "Mrs. Bingley meant her sister."

"My wife is her sister." Wes put an arm around Mary and drew her closer to his side.

His mother pressed her lips together and shook her head. "He will never change, will he?"

"I hope he does not," Mary said.

"Neither do I," Lady Matlock admitted.

"I sent the pralines to the kitchen," Kitty said. "Is everything else ready?"

"Everything is just as it should be," Lydia assured her. "Lady Matlock, Mary, and I have been busy." She gave Kitty a hug. "You will love it."

To everyone's surprise, the closeness that had sprung to life between Lydia and Mary while they were staying at Matlock House all those years ago had only deepened over the years. No longer was Mary the sister without a confidant. Lydia had become that, and Lady Matlock had taken to mothering both of them quite easily. Of course, Lady Matlock was delighted to have two daughters, but even more thrilling to her was that at least one of the two former Miss Bennets, namely Lydia, was as eager to see a match made or a scheme set in motion as Lady Matlock was, while the other former Miss Bennet assisted her in keeping her eldest son on his toes. Everything was, as Lydia had said, just as it should be.

"Would you care to join us for a drink in the drawing room or would you rather go straight up to get ready for dinner?" Lady Matlock asked Kitty.

"I think I would like to dress." Her gaze shifted to Georgiana.

"After you have greeted my wife properly," Alfred inserted. He tipped his head toward the stairs. "Lorcan can have a drink. It takes him far less time to dress."

"Kitty might need help dressing," Wes whispered in Alfred's ear.

"She will have far better success if Georgie is helping her," Alfred retorted.

Wes guffawed. "Ah, Young Alfred, you have learned well." He threw one arm around Alfred's shoulders while he still held his wife close to his other side with his other arm. "Come along. We will go see Richard."

Richard stood at the door to the drawing room.

"Just because I am not throwing myself into the milieu does not mean I am absent."

"I did not see you," Wes said.

Richard shook his head and turned back to the drawing room. On occasion, he walked with the slightest of limps, and his eyesight had never fully returned. However, he was in all other aspects like he had always been, and seeing him standing at the door to the drawing room, observing all that was going on, made Darcy smile. That was how Richard had been when they were growing up. He was an observer before he was a man of action. It was just that his ability to observe without being noticed was excellent. Therefore, most only saw him act.

For an hour, the drawing room hummed with conversation, and then, once everyone was dressed for dinner, the room fell silent as Lord Matlock rose and gave a nod to Mr. Bennet, who joined him.

"Tonight, we raise our glasses and celebrate the union of Mr. and Mrs. Bennet," Lord Matlock began. "While the world looked on and thought that the Bennets had been dealt a grievous hand of five daughters, leaving Mr. Bennet without an heir, God was blessing us all." He turned to Mr. Bennet. "Thank you for fathering five lovely daughters. Our lives have been made the richer for them."

There was a hearty *Hear! Hear!* that went around the room.

"Mrs. Bennet," Mr. Bennet said, extending his hand to his wife, who came to his side and took it, "and myself have been just as blessed as you have been. I always knew that my daughters would marry well for they were all – every one of them – just as pretty as their mother."

"Oh, Mr. Bennet," Mrs. Bennet said with a blush.

"They still are," Mr. Bennet added, causing another *Hear! Hear!* to go around the room. "However, I never expected that they would marry so well as they have. It is not everyone whose daughter becomes a real lady." He dipped his head in Mary's direction. "We are so pleased that you still gather to celebrate this day when our family began, but we do not wish to forget that today also marks the beginnings of two other families. Therefore, we will begin by raising a glass to Lorcan and Kitty and Alfred and Georgiana who married on this day four years ago. May your families and those of all gathered be as blessed as ours."

"To family," Darcy said and the others repeated.

"And now we will go in for dinner," Lord Matlock said. "Both Langley families will, of course, join us in going in first."

Darcy put his arm around Elizabeth and drew her back as the others formed a processional. He watched each couple leave the room. Lord and Lady Matlock, Mr. and Mrs. Bennet, Kitty and Lorcan, Georgiana and Alfred, Jane and Bingley...

He turned to find Richard and Lydia, as well as Mary and Wes waiting.

"You are after Jane, Elizabeth," Lydia said.

They had always gone into this dinner by the age of each Bennet daughter. The wealth, rank, and title of the ladies' husband did not matter at this feast.

"I was just enjoying watching everyone," Darcy said. "It still amazes me how my life changed because I went to Hertfordshire with Bingley when I had no desire to do so."

"Do you remember how you expected to disappoint your family's expectations by marrying Elizabeth?" Richard asked.

Darcy's eyes narrowed. "I would rather not discuss the ignorance of my former way of thinking, but yes, I do."

"You were wrong," Richard said with a grin.

Wes chuckled.

"Yes, I was," Darcy agreed. "Must you continue to bring that up?"

"You are so rarely wrong to such an astonishing degree," Wes said. "We must occasionally remind you of it."

"I truly do not think that is necessary."

"I think it is," Bingley said from the doorway where he and Jane stood waiting. "You are nearly always right, so it is nice to remember now and again that you are not, in fact, perfect. However, I will remind you gentlemen that it was Darcy's willingness to correct his erroneous way of thinking and his determination to marry Elizabeth that helped all of us find our own happiness."

Darcy chuckled. "You know, Bingley, you do not get enough credit for your wisdom."

"No, I do not," Bingley agreed with a laugh.

"Very well," Wes said. "We owe Darcy a debt of gratitude."

Darcy shook his head. "No, actually, you do not

owe it to me. It was Bingley who made me see reason."

"I have been repaid," Bingley said. "My sister is very happily Lady Broadhurst."

"How are your sister and her family?" Elizabeth asked.

"They are quite well, according to the last letter I received from Caroline," Lydia said.

"Yes, I had the same sort of news," Jane agreed.

The group moved into the dining room, and while Jane and Lydia discussed what they had heard of Lady Broadhurst, Sir Matthew, and their daughter and son, Darcy lifted his wife's fingers to his lips and thanked the Lord for the many blessings he had received as a result of marrying Elizabeth.

Before You Go

If you enjoyed this book, be sure to let others know by leaving a review.

~*~*~

Want to know when other Leenie books will be available?

You can always know what's new with my books by subscribing to my mailing list.

(There will, of course, be a thank you gift for joining because I think my readers are awesome!)

Book News from Leenie Brown

(bit.ly/LeenieBBookNews)

~*~*~

Turn the page to read an excerpt of another one of Leenie's books

His Inconvenient Choice Excerpt

If you like Pride and Prejudice variation series such as the Marrying Elizabeth series, I have written a couple of others including the Choices series. Below is an excerpt from His Inconvenient Choice, which is book 3 in that series and stars Kitty Bennet as the heroine.

CHAPTER 1

January 1, 1812

Colonel Richard Fitzwilliam unfolded the small piece of paper that had been tucked into his pocket as he left Netherfield after the wedding breakfast. He shook his head. Two cousins and a friend married all within the space of two weeks was enough to set anyone's world on end. It was also the sort of thing that made him contemplate his own future. Such thoughts often made his breathing feel forced. He drew a deep breath, trying to rid his body of the feeling of being crushed, but it was only slightly helpful. He knew that his future was not to be so happy as those of his cousins and Bingley. He was not free to choose where he wished. His marriage would be one of convenience; his father would see to that.

He looked surreptitiously at the paper in his palm, not wishing to draw attention to it from the others in the carriage. The drawing there brought a smile to his lips and a pang of regret to his heart. Forget-me-nots graced the lid of a box from which spilled strands of pearls and chains of gold. He folded the drawing again and slipped it back into his pocket. If his heart could make his choice for him instead of his father, Kitty Bennet would be his choice. She had stolen his heart when she shivered in the wind on the street in front of the milliner's shop as she insisted on being introduced to him as Katherine. Upon further acquaintance, she had proven to be a lady who shared many of his same interests and who made him feel at ease. She expected no more from him than to be himself. He did not need to be a military leader or the son of an earl. She was interested in his wooden creations — and not as a lady who was trying to make a favourable impression on a gentleman. No, she listened with interest and animation. She had even sketched a few designs that he might like to use.

"If you could wait but a year," she had said as they strolled the perimeter of the ballroom last evening, "then your inheritance would be yours."

"He will not allow me to be free. He will insist on my marrying before he gives me one farthing more than I have," he had replied. Her eyes had filled with tears that she refused to shed, and his heart had broken a bit more at the thought of a life without her. "If I could wait," he had whispered, "I would wait a thousand years for you."

She had smiled sadly at him and said, "And I would wait for you."

He ran his gloved finger over the drawing in the pocket of his coat. "Do not forget me," she had said as she had slipped it into his pocket when he was taking his leave of her. He knew he would never forget her. His hand closed around the paper.

"You are looking rather pensive, Colonel," said Caroline Bingley. "Are they pleasant thoughts?"

"Not all of them," he said as he turned to look

out the window. If the weather had not been so foul, he would have refused Hurst's offer to travel with him.

"That is a pity," said Louisa. "I prefer to think on pleasant things whenever possible."

"As do I," said Richard, "but it is not always possible."

"A colonel must have many unpleasant things to consider," added Caroline.

"He must," said Richard. "However, I was not thinking as a colonel but as a mere man."

Hurst snorted at the comment. "Do leave him be, Caroline."

"I was only attempting to pass the time in conversation," she replied with a huff. "The light is too poor for anything else."

"I find a quiet nap a most refreshing way to pass a trip," replied Hurst.

"How dull," said Caroline.

"Not at all," said Richard. "I find I would like to close my eyes. It has been a busy two days."

Hurst nodded. "You were out with your men yesterday, were you not?"

"I put them through a few drills to test them. Those who passed were allowed to attend the ball.

Those who did not pass were confined to quarters for the evening." It had been his plan, and a successful one, to keep Wickham from the ball. He would take every opportunity afforded him by his position to ensure that Wickham had less pleasure than he desired. It was the one pleasure he received from his duty.

"And, I believe, you danced every dance, did you not?" asked Louisa.

"All save one." His heart pinched, for that one had been set aside to stroll with Kitty.

"Oh, Hurst, you are right. I do believe a nap must be had. What with an early morning yesterday for the colonel, a night of dancing, and another early start to the day today, he must be very tired." She turned to Caroline. "It would be unkind of us to keep him from his rest."

"I thank you," said Richard with a bow of his head. Then added, "I am indeed rather tired," as he settled back and closed his eyes.

Conversation with anyone at present would be unpleasant; with Caroline Bingley, it would be even more so. His fingers once again sought that slip of paper in his pocket. Finding it, he allowed his mind to wander to the lady who had given it to him, and with a deep exhale, he attempted to find some peace in sleep.

~*~*~*~*~*~

"Mr. Darcy, might I have a word with you?" Kitty turned from the window where she had been watching the Hursts' carriage drive away. There were not many wedding guests remaining, and she knew that both she and the Darcys would leave soon.

"Certainly," replied Darcy. He had not had very many opportunities to speak with Kitty. She seemed to avoid him whenever possible, and so her request surprised him. He watched her twist her fingers together and bite her lip, signs that he had learned through watching his wife indicated she was nervous.

"I have a little bit of money and expect to receive some more." She resisted the urge to duck her head and hide from him. His presence had always unsettled her. She was sure he was at any moment going to scold her for some foolishness. She knew she had no reason to feel so, but she did. However, she also knew that he would best be able to advise her, and so she straightened her shoulders and continued. "I have sold some designs to Mrs. Havelston, and she has requested some more. I have not signed them with my name, and it is to be a secret arrangement." The words rushed from her. "I would like to invest it. I know that you can earn money with money, but I do not know how to do it, and I am not a gentleman, which limits me."

He smiled at her. "That sounds like a wise thing to do."

Her brows drew together. "It does?"

"Indeed." He smiled at her again and was rewarded with a small smile in return.

She withdrew a small velvet pouch from her reticule. "It is really very little. It may not be enough to invest yet, but I dare not place it in my father's strongbox, for if something happens to him, I do not wish to explain it to Mr. Collins."

Darcy took the bag from her and slipped it into his pocket. "I shall care for it. You will keep a record of what you have given me, and I will do the same. You know how to do this?"

She pursed her lips and drew her brows together. "I will have my father show me."

"Very good."

"Mr. Darcy, could we save some time and trouble if I request my uncle to give the money to you?"

She twisted her hands again. "He regularly receives payments from Mrs. Havelston for her orders, so no one would suspect she is paying me if she gives it to him. And if he meets with you, no one would question the activity."

He nodded. The thought she had put into her plans impressed him. If he were perfectly honest with himself, he would not have thought her capable of such well-thought-out plans. She had, on the occasions when he had been in her company before his marriage to Elizabeth, struck him as flighty and silly. He chided himself. He had not noted such behaviour since their arrival last week. "I understand. This is an arrangement that is to be private."

"Very. If anyone was to learn that I was earning money…"

"I understand," said Darcy. "Do you have a plan in mind for the money?"

The tears that had been threatening all morning sprang to her eyes, and her cheeks flushed in embarrassment.

"You do not have to tell me," Darcy said quietly.

She shook her head. "I have a foolish notion that will probably be unsuccessful, but your cousin should not be forced to give up what he loves. I thought perhaps I could help him find a way to be happy." She shrugged. "If not, then the money can be added to my portion, which will be of assistance to me when I need to set up my own establishment. I do not wish to live solely on the charity of my relations."

"You do not plan to marry?" Darcy asked in some surprise.

The tears once again gathered in her eyes, and she blinked against them as she shook her head. "I had hoped," she said softly.

His eyes followed her gaze toward the window and the drive at Netherfield. "One must not lose hope, Miss Kitty. Circumstances can change."

She drew a deep breath and released it slowly as she steadied her emotions. Then, she gave him as much of smile as she could manage. "While I own that it is not an utter impossibility, I think it highly unlikely."

He nodded as she thanked him and went to join her father, who was saying his farewells to Elizabeth and Jane. Elizabeth caught Darcy's eye and gave him a questioning look and in response, he shrugged and smiled.

"You look troubled, my dear," she said as she slipped her arm into his and waved to her father's carriage.

"I believe I am," he said as he assisted her into their carriage. Then, he gave one more wave to Bingley and climbed in beside her. Shaking the rain from his hat, he set it on the bench across from them before tucking a blanket across their laps. "Shall we pass the journey as we did on our wedding day?"

She giggled. "I should like that very much, Mr. Darcy, but not until you tell me what has you troubled. I shall not be distracted by your sweet kisses until I know all."

"Is that a fact?" He leaned over and kissed her softly.

She smiled and pushed at his chest. "I would like nothing better than to be distracted so pleasantly, sir, but I am afraid my mind will not be settled until you have told me about what you and Kitty were speaking."

He gave her a quick kiss before she could stop him. "Very well. Your sister has asked me to help her with her finances. It seems she has sold some designs and intends to sell some more, and she wishes to have her earnings invested."

"And this has you troubled?" Elizabeth's brows furrowed as one eyebrow rose in disbelief. "Is it that she is earning money which has concerned you?"

He chuckled and shook his head. "Her selling designs and wishing to invest is not what has me troubled. I asked her what she intended to do with the money, and she nearly cried." He stroked Elizabeth's cheek with his thumb and smiled sadly at her. "Based on her answers and my cousin's strange behaviour last night and this morning, I believe she has had her heart broken by my uncle." He first gave Elizabeth's pursed lips a kiss and then the deep furrow between her brows. "She wishes to help Richard with her money. She does not wish to see him forced to give up what he loves. She also said she no longer intends to marry." He wrapped his arms around Elizabeth and drew her closer as he saw sadness enter her eyes. "And that has me troubled, for I do not wish to see either her or Richard give up whom they love."

"What can be done?" Elizabeth peeked up at him from where her head rested on his shoulder.

"I do not know. My uncle will make it challenging. He wishes a marriage of advantage for Richard, one that will strengthen his political ties and increase Richard's wealth. It will take some thought. However, nothing can be done at present." He kissed her forehead again. "And now, Mrs. Darcy, since I have told you all that is troubling me, I believe I may now distract you with kisses."

She wrapped her arms around his neck. "I believe you must." And eagerly, he obliged.

~*~*~*~*~*~

Richard handed his hat and coat to Harrison, the Matlocks' butler, and slipped into his mother's sitting room to greet her.

Lady Matlock held him close for a moment. "I am happy to see you safely returned to me. Will you be staying?" She took a seat on a settee and motioned for him to join her.

"I have no choice. I do not wish to impose on Darcy or Rycroft as they are settling in with their wives."

"There is BayLeafe," his mother said softly. BayLeafe was the small estate just outside of town which was part of the inheritance that should come to him through his mother should his father see fit to give it him.

He shook his head at her offering.

"Your father is in quite a state what with both of your cousins marrying outside of what is proper." She reached up and brushed his hair back from his forehead. "He is not all bad, you know. He has been good to me. He is just set in his ways."

"Do you love him?" Richard's voice was soft.

"I suppose I do," she replied. "It is possible to become friends and then more even when you begin as near strangers." She took his hand. "I cannot say I have never wished for more or for another, for I did at first, but now, I cannot imagine my life in any other way."

Richard nodded and placed the small folded drawing in her hand. "You would have liked her," he said as she unfolded the paper. Where his father blustered, his mother spoke softly. Where his father was arrogant, she demonstrated grace and humility. They were in many ways as opposed as darkness and light.

She lay the drawing on her lap, a hand resting on her heart. "It is very well done. Who is she?"

He shook his head and took the paper from her

lap. "It matters not, for it shall never be." He rose and went to the window. "She has neither wealth nor significant connections beyond our family."

Lady Matlock came to stand near him. "She is connected to our family?"

He nodded. "Her sisters are the new Mrs. Darcy and Lady Rycroft." He turned toward her. "And that is not the worst of it. A third sister is the new Mrs. Bingley." He watched her struggle with how to accept this information. He knew she loved him and would wish him only to be happy, but she also held to some of the same ideas regarding marriage as her husband. It was not only his father who wished him to make a good match. He tucked the paper in his pocket. "As I said, it matters not, for it shall never be. My heart is of little importance."

Raised voices could be heard from somewhere down the hall.

"Your aunt Catherine is here," his mother said in answer to his questioning look. "Anne is with her but has taken to her room, whether it is due to ill health or a need to avoid her mother, I am uncertain."

Just then, Lady Catherine stomped into the sitting room. "He is as unreasonable as ever!"

"I am not being unreasonable. You are being daft. To accept such connections into the family without some censure? And after he did not marry Anne as we had planned?" Lord Matlock threw his hands up as if unable to fathom the thoughts.

"It would be better for Anne to marry someone with higher connections," said Lady Catherine, "a peer or the son of a peer." Her eyes came to rest on Richard. "Even a second son would do."

A sly smile spread slowly across Lord Matlock's face. "That is an idea. It would keep all the land holding within the family." He clapped his hands together and rubbed them back and forth. "I shall have my solicitor draw up the arrangement. Shall we have the wedding in two months? I do think that would give enough time to find him a replacement with his unit and ready the necessary items for the release of his inheritance, but I will have to defer to my solicitor and man of business for advice before we finalize the date." He leveled a hard glare at Richard. "Any objection shall be met with a significant, if not permanent breach. Do I make myself clear?"

Richard shook his head in disbelief. "I am no more to you than that?"

"On the contrary," said his father, "you are of great significance, and that is why your future must be secured. Were something to ever happen to your brother, you would need to secure the title with an appropriate heir, one with an acceptable lineage."

Richard's jaw clenched. "So I am a well-bred horse in your stable then, whose only expectation is to sire the next prize stallion. And if I do not, I, like that horse, shall be turned out to work alongside the other workhorses on the estate."

His father's eyes narrowed. "Not on my estates." His voice held more than a little warning.

Richard stepped closer and pulled himself up to his full height, which was two inches taller than his father. "And if you turn me out and something happens to my brother, then where will your precious title fall? Ah, yes, to your brother." The comment caused the reaction he desired. His father took a step back and his face paled slightly. "Two weeks," Richard said. "I ask two weeks to consider your offer, sir."

"What is there to consider?" said Lady Catherine.

"The value of my life," Richard snarled. He

moved toward the door, but his mother's hand on his arm forestalled him.

"I will see you again?" Her eyes were filled with fear.

"At least once more," he murmured as he kissed her cheek before leaving the room and instructing that his things be readied for a journey.

Acknowledgments

There are many who have had a part in the creation of this story. Some have read and commented on it. Some have proofread for grammatical errors and plot holes. Others have not even read the story and a few, I know, will never read it. However, their encouragement and belief in my ability, as well as their patience when I became cranky or when supper was late or the groceries ran low, was invaluable.

And so, I would like to say *thank you* to Zoe, Rose, Kristine, Ben, and Kyle, as well as my patrons on Patreon and the readers who faithfully read all those Thursday posts on my blog. I feel blessed by your help, support, and understanding.

I have not listed my dear husband in the above group because, to me, he deserves his own special thank you, for, without his somewhat pushy insistence that I start sharing my writing, none of my writing goals and dreams would have been met.

~*~*~

For those who might be interested in some of the visual inspiration I used while writing this book — I have a Pinterest board for that.

Other Leenie B Books

You can find all of Leenie's books at this link
bit.ly/LeenieBBooks
where you can explore the collections below

~*~

Other Pens, Mansfield Park

~*~

Touches of Austen

~*~

Dash of Darcy and Companions Collection

~*~

Marrying Elizabeth Series

~*~

Sweet Possibilities, A Darcy and Elizabeth Variations Collection

~*~

Willow Hall Romances

~*~

The Choices Series

~*~

Darcy Family Holidays

~*~

Darcy and... An Austen-Inspired Collection

~*~

Nature's Fury and Delights (A Sweet Regency Novelettes Series)

About the Author

Leenie Brown has always been a girl with an active imagination, which, while growing up, was both an asset, providing many hours of fun as she played out stories, and a liability, when her older sister and aunt would tell her frightening tales. At one time, they had her convinced Dracula lived in the trunk at the end of the bed she slept in when visiting her grandparents!

Although it has been years since she cowered in her bed in her grandparents' basement, she still has an imagination which occasionally runs away with her, and she feeds it now as she did then — by reading!

Her heroes, when growing up, were authors, and the worlds they painted with words were (and still are) her favourite playgrounds! Now, as an adult, she spends much of her time in the Regency world, playing with the characters from her favourite Jane Austen novels and those of her own creation.

When she is not traipsing down a trail in an attempt to keep up with her imagination, Leenie resides in the beautiful province of Nova Scotia with her two sons and her very own Mr. Brown (a wonderful mix of all the best of Darcy, Bingley, and Edmund with a healthy dose of the teasing Mr. Tilney and just a dash of the scolding Mr. Knightley).

Connect with Leenie

E-mail:
LeenieBrownAuthor@gmail.com
Facebook:
www.facebook.com/LeenieBrownAuthor
Blog:
leeniebrown.com
Patreon:
https://www.patreon.com/LeenieBrown
Subscribe to Leenie's Mailing List:
Book News from Leenie Brown
(bit.ly/LeenieBBookNews)

www.ingramcontent.com/pod-product-compliance
Lightning Source LLC
Chambersburg PA
CBHW060901250626
47159CB00008B/2827